Antonija Mežnarić

IT EATS US FROM THE INSIDE

Antonija Mežnarić

IT EATS US FROM THE INSIDE

EDITED BY
Vesna Kurilić

COVER BY
Antonio Filipović

ISBN
ebook 978-953-8360-18-3
paperback 978-953-8360-19-0

First Edition

Rijeka, 2022.
shtriga.com
shtrigabooks@gmail.com

ANTONIJA MEŽNARIĆ

IT EATS US FROM THE INSIDE

SHTRIGA

CONTENTS

CHAPTER 1

THE PUNGENT STENCH OF the sea hit Doris in full force as soon as she got out of the safety of her air-conditioned car. Unprepared for it, her gag reflex kicked in, and she had to force her lunch to stay where it was, digesting in her stomach rather than splattering all over her. The smell was wrong, oily and heavy, with an unnatural acidic taste to it. It reminded her of the time she used to clean fish for lunch on the dock if that fish had already been rotten instead of freshly caught. The worst of it was that the small parking lot was situated on the waterfront which made it all the more inescapable and stronger. It even managed to distract her from the fact that, outside of the car, she was now exposed to the unforgiving blazing sun.

"Fuck, this is horrible," she heard her wife say, by the passenger's seat doors. Erika's face was scrunched in distaste, locs hidden under the headscarf she'd fastened before getting out. "Do they know why it smells like that?"

"Have no idea, mom also didn't know." Doris had seen some of the reports, news, and panicked conspiracies on the social media hellscapes about this pollution, but didn't expect it to be like this. Her most reliable source had been her mother, but she, also, didn't live here anymore, so she couldn't know how it actually was.

The very few docked boats lulled lazily on the surface, looking old and unkempt. The scarcity surprised her—though it shouldn't have. She doubted anyone ever went out in them; what would be the point without edible fish or a chance to swim? To hop onto the closest island? The bald, rocky, brown side of the Pag island was just opposite the coast, its length parallel to the town, blocking the view at the horizon. But she wasn't sure how far the toxicity had spread or even if there was anyone here who hadn't already run away. There were apparently people living here still—she was here precisely because of one stubborn individual—not that she could understand that need, especially now, when she was inhaling the diseased sea into her lungs.

The view was also just... wrong. Instead of the beautiful stretch of aquamarine, there was something, right there, on the surface, but she couldn't be sure what her eyes were seeing. Curious, she came closer to the edge of the parking lot and leaned towards the sea, murky with a dense layer of muck. It covered the sea from the shallows to the depths—almost as if someone had filled out plastic bags with a light red substance resembling diluted blood, and then tossed them overboard. Only, there were countless of these bags on the surface, an infinity of them, impossible for anyone to have created this sort of detritus. It must've been the bacteria doing something to the sea flora. The sourness permeating from it invaded her nostrils, tickling her palate with its foulness. The tuna sandwich she'd eaten on the trip was continually threatening with a comeback. She put the palm over her nose and mouth, but it was like trying to close down a disemboweling cut with a band-aid.

Doris moved away from the edge, suddenly worried

she would lose balance and fall. In normal circumstances, that would've been the preferred outcome—once upon a time, she used to dive from here to cool out from the summer heat. After a full day on the road, she wanted nothing more than that sea of old, for her and Erika to strip off and go on a swim. This mucus-filled stinking soup didn't have that same lure.

She turned her back to it, looking towards the town that had seen her growing up and becoming a teen, before her mother finally saw reason and took her away from it.

Karlobag stayed just as she had remembered it, with a row of small, sturdy houses along a road, growing like mushrooms up towards the mountain that loomed over the town with its spikes and curves. Velebit—a slumbering giant—tolerated Karlobag situated at the foot of its slopes.

Erika had already unloaded the car taking out their bags—not much, only two, and both small. Only one more car, besides theirs, was parked at the lot, alongside a black van with tinted windows. Doris went to the parking meter she remembered from her teens, with a small solar panel powering it. Its metallic blue was rusted over with time, rain, and salt. The display showed flickering broken lines, turning the words into unreadable gibberish. Only the word PLEASE was clear enough. It sounded desperate, pleading with Doris, and the discomfort crept over her.

"You know something is very, very wrong when the parking meter is broken during the summer season," Erika said, looking at Doris' attempts to get it to work. No matter how many times she tapped the touchscreen, it stayed a flickering mess, and when she checked her watch it didn't show that it recognized new devices she could connect to. That part wasn't that surprising; she'd left a long time ago and it was obvious they hadn't changed the machine, updated it with the modern times.

"Yes, well, this was never a popular destination." Doris looked over to the houses on the other side of the road, the first line of the town. It wasn't a complete truth. While the town had lost a lot when the highway was built—a long time ago—connecting Croatia's north and south but bypassing Karlobag completely, it was still on the coast and, as such, a tourist destination regardless. It had been especially popular with bikers since the old road, the Magistrala—which had been the first connective tissue of the north and south before the highway—was famous for its dangerous serpentines and beautiful views, marking Karlobag a special place to stop while on the road. There were also always a lot of people from towns on the other side of the mountain, who wanted to go to the beach over the weekend and this had been the closest spot. Or those who had families here and had inherited houses from dead relatives, though this group always lived somewhere else and only came here when on vacation. It just wasn't that hot of a destination as some other coastal towns on the highway, or the islands. Like, for example, how its neighbor island Pag used to be—and probably still was—a true tourist trap, always choking on crowds and a rich nightlife.

"Well, if there's anyone who still cares, they can fine us," Doris said, giving up on the meter. She reached out and took Erika's hand in hers, something she didn't get to do when she used to live here. Like that, the two of them crossed the street. The first building they came across was the restaurant where her family used to come for pizza nights, now empty and closed, its terrace just a concrete spot, devoid of tables, chairs, and patrons.

Houses had their windows closed, blinds firmly shut. Parts of Karlobag which were close to the coast were cramped, houses close to one another, the better to protect them when the strong northern wind came crashing from the mountain to the sea. It meant that, during the summers, it used to be impossible to walk the narrow cobbled paths without seeing someone's living room; doors wide open, uncaring for strangers passing by. There had always been sounds following her—television turned on or people's conversations—but now not a mouse could be heard. Only the steps the two of them made.

The town had that winter aura Doris was also used to. When it looked abandoned and dead—when all of the restaurants were closed and nothing operated except maybe two shops—but was only actually hibernating until spring, when it slowly started to wake up, waiting for the first guests to arrive.

Now, if she had to compare it to anything, it would be a patient in a coma, hooked to failing life support.

It wasn't long before they trudged to the two-storey, ash-gray house, tall, long and unremarkable. Doris paused in front of the red door, her left hand grasping the bag strap over her shoulder, her right still holding Erika's. She thought she was ready. After a flight and most of a day spent on the road and after weeks of discussion, first with her mother, then with her wife, it should've been much easier to knock on the door. This was the end of it all, the travel, the tired fights, the nausea-inducing uncertainty.

Yet, the cherry red door sounded the alarm in her mind. If they opened, it wouldn't be the end. It would be the beginning of something she wasn't sure she wanted to have any role in.

The skin at the back of her sweat-slicked neck prickled. She slowly turned around, looking at the house behind her back—the old Danica's place. The old woman had always been kind towards her and always ready to entertain Doris with her tales—collected and shared through generations of her family—even when the woman started to get lost in her head. Old Danica was now surely dead, even though Doris half expected to see her at her door, with a greeting smile. To welcome her back home. The blinds on the ground floor were shut so tight that not even sunlight could pass, but on the first floor there was an open window and, instead of the ancient woman Doris fondly remembered, a bearded man was leaning over, smoking. Doris knew Danica had a son, but he had been living in Germany with his family and rarely came to visit, so she wouldn't be able to recognize him if it were him. And the ages didn't match—this man looked to be in his fifties, and she was pretty certain the son was now much older than that. Grandson? Some other relative?

Whoever he was, he had a real, old-school cigarette in his mouth, the one with tobacco rolled in paper. It came with a slight shock to Doris, unsure when was the last time she'd seen one of those. She thought it had been banned in all of Europe, but then again, Croatia was always hanging on a precipice of the so-called West. The man was watching Erika and her, a bit bored, like they were a show on TV he accidentally glimpsed while channel surfing. Erika shot him a short greeting, in Croatian, but the man didn't reply, only took a drag, so Doris didn't bother to be polite.

But having an audience gave her the much-needed push towards the door. She was no one's spectacle. Her troubles were not for show.

She knocked three times and, thankfully, didn't have to wait too long before the door opened. And just like that, without much pomp and a bit anticlimactic, she was face to face with her father for the first time after seven years.

Her father was always thin and willowy, fit from all the hiking and the swimming, but now, his body had lost all its fat, turning into a skeleton with skin. His face was gaunt, the icy blue eyes sunken and feverish. He'd lost most of his corn-yellow hair and was almost bald, but not completely. A few tufts, here and there, still grew out of his scalp. He hadn't been a young man when she was born, so she'd been expecting to see an old man, but it wasn't the years that have laid ruin over his body.

The scaly clusters of spots were growing on his skin, sickly and gray, glistening with some sort of moisture. He was riddled with them—bursting across his forehead, neck, shoulders, and arms—as much as she could see.

"I told you to come alone," he said without a greeting, his burning gaze fixed on Erika. Anger surged in Doris, a flame that didn't need much stoking to blaze like a forest fire. She was soaked in her own sweat and sunscreen, stiff from a long trip, nauseous from the smells of the sea and, not to mention, reluctant to be here in the first place, and this is how he welcomed them? Well, he can turn into a sardine and die in the toxic waste of the sea, as far as she was concerned.

But before she could tell him that and turn around, Erika put a hand on her shoulder and said: "She wouldn't be here were it not for me. I would show a bit of respect if I was you. Or maybe she was right all along and this was a waste of time." Her beautiful dark brown eyes were unflinching while she faced her father-in-law, the one she'd met only once, on their wedding day.

"Time you don't have very much of, I would say."

Doris' father squinted at Erika, mouth shrinking into one thin line Doris recognized as a sign of frustration. That was the look he used to give her when she did or said something he didn't agree with, which was almost anything and everything from the moment she became a teen and stopped being the starry-eyed kid who worshiped the ground he walked on.

For a moment she thought he would say something unforgivable to Erika, giving Doris an excuse to flip him off and fuck off from this living carcass of a town, but he deflated, turning slightly so they could enter the house.

"I just didn't think it smart for my daughter to drag you into this mess, but you are both grown women, do what you want. I don't care."

It wasn't an apology, but it was probably the closest thing they would get from him. It would be easier for the sky to turn into an ocean, than for Doris' father to admit he was wrong. This was a mistake, but she already agreed to do this, so there was no point in turning around at this point. Especially not when Erika was smoothly bypassing her, entering the house.

Inside, another smell assaulted Doris, this one an easily recognizable aroma of decay, damp walls, rotten wood, fungi, and dust. The living room was littered with carefully stacked old books, some piles as high as her hips. At the wall, her great-grandparents' ancient armoire looked worse for wear, white paint flaking off in tiny scraps. At least her father had thrown out the old pink couch permanently stained with blood and other secretions she didn't want to think about. Instead, there was a sleek, leathery three-seater. In front of it, with his legs stretched out, the mangy old mutt slept, with no reaction even with two strangers in the house. She would've thought he was dead, if not for the silent snores and twitchy legs of a dreaming dog.

"Stribor is deaf. Ignore him," her father said, pointing at the snoring dog, before disappearing inside the small kitchenette. Stribor's brownish fur was peppered with white hairs, at least at the places it still grew. The dog, Doris noticed with a pang, was also riddled with clusters of unnatural scaly growth, greasy in the light of the lamp. She was suddenly aware of the heavy stagnant air, the closed windows and doors, the lack of air-conditioning, and there was a part of her that wanted to cry, but she blinked the need away. For Erika, who was watching her with sad, concerned eyes.

Carefully stepping over Stribor—so as not to disturb the poor animal—she sat at the edge of the leathery couch, her wife at her side.

Her father came back with two bottles of cold water from the fridge. The chill on her palm was refreshing, and she had to fight off the urge to rub the bottle on the heated skin of her head and neck. He sat opposite them, after cleaning up the stack of books from the chair. It wobbled on the floor, dangerously close to crashing down.

For a few moments, the three of them were only sitting in silence; intently watching each other, the dog's heavy breathing the only sound.

"Mom says it's not dangerous as long as we're not in prolonged contact with the sea," Doris finally broke the silence. It was a hollow statement. The damage was already done, people got infected before they even knew that something was in the sea, changing it.

"To think there was a time we were worried about getting *Escherichia coli* like those stupid bastards in the South," her father spat out, scratching a spot of gray on his cheek. "Ended up with this shit instead. If only it spread across the whole Adriatic and the Mediterranean, no, everywhere, maybe somebody would do something."

"I heard they're still doing testing and research—" Erika said, only to be rudely cut off.

"*They*? Who are they?" Father scoffed. "Government? Which one? The Croatian one is useless, you know that, or you wouldn't have moved out. Those sorry scraps of the European Union? You know it's in shambles, fighting to stay relevant."

"The Americans," Doris said. She uncapped the bottle and took a long sip, enjoying her father's glower. "At least that's what I heard. Mom says she read somewhere there's some US-funded research going on."

"Oh, and some corporate-sponsored research must mean we're going to be saved just right about now. You watched too much of their propaganda as a kid, they're not superheroes."

"And you are too cynical," she said. "Someone is surely doing something. Even if we can't." The brightest Croatia had to offer were smart enough to move away given the chance. And those who stayed probably didn't have the equipment necessary to work on—she would bet her right hand that was the case.

"Why would they?" her father said, with broken, raspy breaths. "They have their own problems. Their companies are setting fire to the ocean floors, maybe they should start from that. Or, as I heard, deadly heat waves are killing thousands each year, shouldn't they be focused on fixing that? I mean, you got a taste of their climate problems yourselves." The memory of the violent storms hit Doris unexpectedly, like a huge flood bursting from the underground. When they'd thought they would die, so far away from home, but simultaneously felt detached from it, as if they were nothing but characters in a Hollywood disaster movie.

Her father continued, following some internal script, as if he were just waiting for the audience so he could get all of his frustrations off his chest. "Meanwhile, each summer, all of Europe erupts in wildfires, eating through the little vegetation we still have. You just missed the two weeks burning of Dalmatia. Ecological catastrophes are happening in all corners of the world, every day, in all shapes. I stopped following and counting them." He stopped his rant to take in some air. "And the earthquakes? We still haven't fixed the damage after the last one that hit us, and it's been *years*. Simply put, why would anyone care about what's happening to *this* town?"

Before she could reply, he heaved into his palms, an ugly and wet cough wrecking his frail body. Out of the corner of her eye, she saw Erika shifting slightly, her arms outstretched towards her father-in-law, only to abort the movement and land in her lap. Doris knew her wife; she was probably torn between helping her father-in-law and leaving him be. Even though their meeting had been brief, seven years ago, she heard enough about Ivo Vrban over time to rightly assume her help wouldn't be accepted. Doris put her hand over Erika's, squeezing it in comfort. Though, if someone had asked her, she couldn't be sure if that was more for her wife's or hers.

After the coughing fit passed, her father's palms were full of mucus slowly dribbling down through his fingers. Before any of them could try and find a tissue, he simply wiped off his hands on his pants, leaving smears all over his worn-out trousers. He was never this uncaring for his personal hygiene, at least not while Doris and her mother lived with him. This was hard to swallow.

They may have a complicated relationship... but that didn't mean she could sit here and feel nothing over his downfall.

"Don't look at me like that." His voice was gruff, face crumpled in disgust. Did he feel the indignity? A proud man once; this state he was in couldn't be easy for him. "Besides, I didn't call you because I think some doctor somewhere will find a cure. There's... another way."

"I know that the doctors can't do much," Doris started, carefully, "but surely you can't think you can find something in... folklore which might help?" She glimpsed at the stacks of books towering around them in messy heaps. Hoarding books wasn't new to him, but there used to be a method to his shelves and he always properly cared for the titles he had. Was this collection of old, leathery spines and brittle yellow paper here because of his frantic search for a cure? And if the answer was yes, what was going on in his head? "This is a disease, bacteria, not one of your tales."

"My tales? None of them are *mine*." There was bitterness in his tone, but also a reverence she knew well. She remembered her father's lectures when she was a child, knew what he would say even before he opened his mouth to reply. "They belong to the communities that tell them, that remember them. I simply collect and preserve." And he's always been so proud of that. "But you know that, better than anyone in this world. Yet you choose to act as if this has nothing to do with you."

Their old quarrels were slowly bubbling up to the surface, threatening to overflow and drown them in a torrent, catching Erika too, who had nothing to do with any of this. Every time they talked, no matter the topic, Doris' father found a way to get back to it, circling back to what he thought was her great betrayal. It was a great serpent eating its own tale. A never-ending discussion. It was the reason she'd stopped talking to him during the last seven years, why she'd never come back to visit him after getting away.

She was too damn tired.

"Why do you think you can find help with... old powers?" She refused to call it a god and wasn't even certain what it was. Except that it was what powered the old tales, gave them meaning, or, maybe, it was the other way around. What people felt existed outside of this world, but didn't know how to properly explain it. So they spun stories and legends which were only a hint of something greater. "I doubt you're talking about folk medicine. It's not like there's a manual for calling on magic." The word *magic* also tasted wrong on her tongue, but it was closer to what she wanted to say. Unless she'd misunderstood him and he actually planned to convert to some South Slavic neo-pagan cult.

"It's happening. Again," he answered, and briefly looked at Erika, uncertainty in his voice. As if he wasn't sure how much could he say in front of Doris' wife, probably thinking she would find him a senile old man.

"You might say I have my own experience with... the supernatural." Erika must've thought the same, promising to believe whatever he had to say and prompting him to speak.

The thin line of an eyebrow, that still existed under the ugly gray growth on his forehead, arched, and Doris knew his curiosity was sparked. If he gets the chance, he'll definitely try to pry out Erika's story.

"There are sightings," his words came out scratchy, as if he had something in his throat blocking the sounds, "of dead Turks floating in the water of Lomivrat, and—"

"I'm sorry, what? Turks?" Erika interrupted in shock.

She leaned towards him, questioning. "I mean, seeing floating people is freaky, but how can anyone know they're Turkish people?" Her eyes flitted over to Doris.

"Because that's the legend," Doris jumped in to explain before her father could. "It's said that, during the Turkish invasion, Lomivrat's locals forced the Turkish forces to fall down the cliffs and into the sea, breaking their necks in the process. That's the explanation behind the name of the place: it, quite literally, 'breaks necks'." She taught for a moment and added, remembering Erika—as a continental Croatian—wasn't as familiar with the geography of Velebit's foothill: "Lomivrat is a small village near Prizna, close to where you go to catch a ferry for Pag."

"It's abandoned now," her father added. "A ghost village full of corpses with broken necks in the sea." Doris wanted to ask who had seen, then, these floating dead, but knew better than to try and find logic, or source, in these types of tales. "And not only that." He turned towards his daughter, his palms grasping at his trousers. The yellow-green spot marred his pants, leaving a sign of his sickness. A pang of panic pricked her heart, but she told it to stay calm. "Hikers are disappearing near Velinac, one of the Velebit's peaks famous in folklore for having fairies," he added for Erika's sake. "Someone said they saw a rolling waterskin full of blood on Magistrala and got into a crash trying to avoid it, and..." A cough shuddered through him for a moment, and Doris' throat constricted. It was just like years ago, when strange sightings kept popping up all over villages and towns of northern Velebit, mostly among scared tourists who thought the locals were somehow messing with them. She knew what he'd say next and already dreaded it.

"People are dreaming of the well, aren't they?" she asked, as soon as he calmed down. He didn't need to say anything; the look on his face—strained as if he were preparing for the possible explosion—told her everything.

Her vision blurred, and she wasn't sure if it was because of travel fatigue or due to her shallow breathing getting the stuffy air into her lungs, or because this was the last topic she wanted to talk about.

The last thing she wanted to revisit on this trip down memory lane.

"I dreamt of it." His words were a bucket of ice dumped over her overheated brain. "It's true," he continued, seeing her shocked face. "I keep dreaming of a long fall down the well, and when my body finally hits the ground, there's something there, in the dark." His eyes twinkled with the fever eating at them. "I think... well, I *know* it's supposed to be gold, but I can't see it clearly. When I try to get closer, a snake blocks the way. That's when I wake up." He paused for a moment, frowning. "And in that one moment, when my brain slips from sleeping to awareness, the real location of the well is right there, on tip of my tongue, but as soon as I try to remember it, to write it down, it's lost, again."

It was as straightforward as any other tale of the lost Roman ninth well on Velebit usually went among the folk narrators. There were eight wells on Velebit that everyone knew about, but there was this last one, the location of which was unknown, with a hidden treasure. You can dream about it but, awake, you can't find it. Sometimes, there's also an imprisoned young woman, and the dreamer, usually a man, can then *and* and get the gold.

It was, also, not how that same tale had happened to

her, when she'd dozed off on a pink couch in front of the TV one fateful night and found herself on the other side of reality, at the damp bottom of the lost, impossible well. There was no treasure. Or, not in the way the elders had believed, thinking, in purely materialist terms, of some hidden Roman jewels and gold.

"Wait, so you think I can help you in some way? With what's been happening? Is that why you begged me to come home?" The thought chilled her. He couldn't be that foolish. What if he was? What if he believed she had a magical way to fix everything—his health, the sea, the town—only for her to refuse out of, what, pride? Just because he knew she was the only one to not only dream of well, but gain its prize too? "You know I have no idea how to get to it." And besides, what did he plan to do, even if she could? She doubted he was after the Roman riches.

You know what he's pursuing, she thought, watching his thin body riddled with unnatural growths, hearing the rasping sounds his breathing made.

His eyes were melting polar ice, face unreadable. It was Erika's turn to put a hand on Doris' thigh, consoling her. Probably aware of what kind of toll it took on Doris to have this conversation.

"Don't be ridiculous," her father finally said, "I know you don't have power." Her relief was brief, bracing herself for his request, whatever that may be.

The ninth well had chosen her, not the other way around, and she was pretty sure that, even if it called her back, it would not have the answers her father wanted. And there was no way, in no world, ever, that she would willingly go back there, to those damp walls closing on her from all sides, and the infinite darkness.

Erika squeezed her thigh. Doris was on the brink of

a panic attack, breathing hard and fast, shaking slightly. Her father didn't notice; he was coughing again.

"I just..." he tried to say, but shot up from the chair instead and ran off in the direction of the bathroom, knocking down a few of his towers of paper Babylon. They could hear the raspy sounds of vomiting. A tremble passed all over Doris and she leaned over her knees, her head in her palms.

"This was a mistake. We shouldn't have come here. Who knows what he thinks I can accomplish? Did the bacteria eat his brain? Make him delusional?" she mumbled. Erika put a hand over her shoulder and budged Doris' face towards herself.

"Honey, your dad is dying," she said once her eyes settled on Doris. Erika's tone carried a sad finality to it. "And no matter how messy your relationship has become, you still love him and you'd carry on the guilt for the rest of your life if you didn't hear him out before he died." It was the argument that had won Doris over, the reason she'd finally succumbed to her mother's urging to accept her father's frantic calls to come visit him.

Erika was right. If he died while Doris was ignoring him, she wouldn't have to deal with complicated grief alone, but also guilt and resentment.

"Erika, I can't help him if he plans to... I don't know, sleep himself to his grave. He's talking about..." She waved her hand around, trying to find the words.

"The mountain god. I know," Erika said, as simple as that. She frowned. "Or is it more accurate to say the mountain as a god? Rather than there being a separate being that simply lives on the... you know what, not important."

"In the end, he will die thinking I've failed him,"

Doris said with a heavy sigh, ignoring Erika's contemplation on gods. They had a much different approach to the impossible. Erika was more like Doris' father in that regard—her teenage experience with a haunted čardak in Bosnia, which simultaneously existed and did not, made her want to understand the supernatural. Doris, on the other hand, did not want to comprehend the power that resided here, in these rocks, peaks, and crevices, and had done a whole lot of work to block out the memory of that night.

"He's desperate." Erika kissed her on the temple, gently. "He probably only wants his daughter close by in his last days. To see you for the last time and, possibly, mend the cracks in your relationship."

"You don't know that," Doris choked out. The sound of flushing water signaled them to finish the conversation. But Erika had one last thing to add before that.

"We took the time off to come here. Use it to hang around, talk with him, and yes, indulge him a bit. Maybe you'll make up, maybe you won't. You'll at least know that you did what you could in the end." *Once he's dead* went unsaid, but Doris knew it was what Erika was thinking.

Her father came back, hunched over. His face was pale, his expression forlorn. The gray scales were accentuated under the light of the lamp, glistening after he'd washed his face.

Even if they found out how to fight against this new bacteria, it was too late for her father. It had damaged him beyond repair. His internal organs were slowly, but steadily, liquifying. First it had been his body fat. Now, organs. And no one knew how to stop it. They only knew that Doris' father had been the first one to show the progression from skin lesions to organ failure.

At least, it was what her mother had told her, keeping informed with his circumstances even when they were long divorced, when it would be so easier to leave him in her past and focus on her future. Doris wasn't certain if she did that for her stubborn daughter, who was refusing to communicate with him, or if she'd felt a misplaced responsibility for him because of his disease and impending death.

He plopped down on the chair—like a tree cut down, falling in the forest where the two of them had been able to hear it. She could feel his malaise in her bones as if she were sharing his sickness.

She sighed, accepting her fate. Erika was right. They had taken time off, they'd come all the way here, and her father was dying. She could at least try to spend some time with him before it happened, even if he only had desperate endeavors.

"Please, I just... I need..." her father croaked, crumbling in on himself, leaving the sentence unfinished. Even if she hadn't already made her decision, that would've broken her resolve. "You're back. And that matters," he finally said. Did he mean it mattered to him in the way Erika believed, only to be with her in his dying days? Or he believed her presence would be some sort of a tipping point in these strange events? "You were chosen once... maybe, again, if you pleaded, if you prayed..."

So it was the other thing. He was not seeking a company, but a mailwoman to the powers above who could, possibly, help him out.

"Alright," Doris said, stiff, hiding her disappointment. He'd said, once, that she was chosen, and yes, that was true. Chosen to be a plaything to something she couldn't comprehend. Why else was she the only one that got the chance to get what she needed, what she wanted, but not someone else in a similar position? She refused to believe she was somehow special. What else could've been the reason if not some cosmic game or an epic coincidence? Not that her father could understand that. He hadn't been lost in the well. Hadn't been woken in a cocoon made of his own melted body. "I can't promise you anything. You know that. But I'll stay for a few days. See what's going on." Try to learn about the disease, find out what was being done in response, and by whom.

Her father didn't smile, but he did nod in gratitude. The bald spot on the top of his head was covered in gray scales. In a trick of the light, as he nodded, it expanded before her eyes, growing like a puddle of discolored diarrhea over the pale pink of the old skin.

CHAPTER 2

DINNER WAS AN AWKWARD affair. Doris and Erika ate on the couch, plates on their knees. They still had some tuna sandwiches from the trip, and Doris' father managed to get them hard cheese from Pag. He couldn't eat solid food, so he had a small jar of baby food which precariously stood on a book stack. Stribor, the dog, had woken up and was now gnawing on his own bone with raw red gums, slowly slurping through the missing teeth in his jaw. She had asked her father why he didn't give Stribor some wet food, to which he only said: "It comforts the dog."

Something on her plate reeked of spoiled food and she discreetly tried to discover what. It couldn't have been the sandwich—unless the tuna had already managed to turn bad during the trip. The cheese gave off the distinctive whiff of mold, but it didn't match that strong smell of rotten meat that permeated her brain. It probably wasn't the food anyway, just the stench of the apartment getting to her, spoiling everything.

Her stomach roiled in distress and she wasn't able to force down more than a few bites. She noticed that Erika had barely touched her food too. Father was miserably putting spoonfuls of orange mush into his mouth, absentmindedly scratching at the patch on his cheek with his free hand. The growth bloomed with dirty white droplets, breaking the surface through the holes his nails left in the scales.

Only the dog seemed content with his meal, his toothless maw chewing the old bone.

Erika made most of the small talk. Asking around how many people were still in town—not many, all who could afford to move away had done it, but that wasn't anything new; that was the case even when Doris had been a child. There was no work to be had in Karlobag for the better part of the year. Only in the summer season, and even that wasn't as rich as it could've been. Did he know how many of them were also diseased? All of them. They'd all contracted the bacteria before they'd even known it existed.

Even babies people brought along to the beach to cool a bit from the blazing summer heat.

"We had a bit of quarantine at the start, but once it was proved you couldn't transmit the bacteria from person to person or by air, it was lifted. And while Pag would be absolutely happy to protect their sea with some underwater wall to make sure it never spreads to them, it's still impossible. Right now, they're throwing a lot of money into some nano filters that are supposed to be like little slimy robot plankton programmed to find and eat the bacteria, but who knows if they'll work, or if it's going to backfire on those stupid rich assholes. They're feeding their own coast with that shit at least. Apparently 'it's already too late for us.'."

They called it *B. scrissa* and no, he had no idea who got *that* idea. Unusual and previously unidentified. It should've been a scientific wonder, heavily researched and documented; instead, it was treated like trash.

There was no way everyone was ignoring it, Doris thought, it was too novel, too destructive to pass under the radar, even if Croatia didn't have the facilities or the people to investigate it properly.

When the two of them managed to convince him that they were done with dinner, even though their plates remained full, he gave Doris a key.

"Your old room has been converted into my office, so I'm afraid you'll have to sleep in the other house."

She glimpsed at Erika's confused face, but only nodded at her father. "What state is it in?"

His hand briefly passed over his bald head, eyes for a moment lost in thought. "It's alright. Maybe a bit dusty. I'd planned on using it as a rental, only, once news broke that you should avoid the sea, it was obvious I wouldn't be getting any guests. Hikers pass through, here and there, so I had some traffic. Not much once it had started to smell like the inside of a whale's carcass."

"You planned on dealing with tourists?" She couldn't imagine that. Or, better said, she could imagine all the scathing one-star reviews piling up on various apps.

"I'm charming when I have to be. Otherwise, I wouldn't have been very good at my job, would I?"

Doris had to suppress a laugh. Talking to the folk storytellers and recording their tales wasn't the same thing as taking care of a rental summer house.

It was all so very weird. Being here again, talking with him, knowing that strange things were happening, but most of all, that he was dying in front of her eyes.

"I would suggest keeping the windows, shutters, and curtains closed at all times. The smell at night becomes even worse and you know that, when the swelter slithers in, it's hard to breathe. And you don't have to worry, you have air-conditioning. I don't use it here, because... I can't handle the cold." He sounded ashamed mentioning it. Doris lightly grasped his upper arm, where a little of his skin still remained untouched.

"It's alright. Get some rest and we'll talk in the morning."

Hopefully. She briefly wondered if he'll have the same dream tonight. She didn't want to think about what dreams she could get, dreading sleep.

"You know, when we went outside of your dad's home, I thought we were going to walk much farther than, er, the exact same house, just to enter at the other side," Erika said when Doris let them in her late uncle's home, now her father's failed rental.

"This used to be one house when my grandparents owned it. They left it to dad and my uncle, and once grandpa died, they split it in half and bricked it in between," she explained, walking across the unrecognizable living room. The cheap, impersonal furniture wasn't the one she remembered but it was exactly what one would expect from a short-term rental. Her finger passed over the TV hanging on the wall, collecting a thick layer of dust like a snowball on the fingertip. She noticed her dad had thrown away the virtual assistant uncle had used, something her father despised.

Her uncle used to have a great chestnut library shelf filled with records from top to bottom; she could still imagine it stretching from one side of the wall to the other. Now, there were no shelves and a generic oil painting of a sailing ship on a calm sea hung on the wall instead.

"Didn't you have a bunch of cousins? You never mentioned living with them, or your uncle, for that matter, just your parents."

"Because I didn't. Grandpa died when I was little, so we moved here then." Her parents used to live in Zagreb; father was employed at the Institute of Ethnology and Folklore Research when he met her mother, a grad student working on her master's in sociology. Doris used to wonder how he'd managed to convince her mother to move from a big city to literal nowhere, but with time, she learned that, when you love someone, you're ready for a compromise. The same way that Erika had followed her now, Doris would follow her no matter where Erika's path would lead her. "If you want to hear even more family drama, my father and my uncle had a huge fight when I was very young. About the house—uncle was very unhappy that dad wanted to come back and live in his own half. Thought he would inherit it all because he'd stayed in Karlobag, taking care of grandfather, while dad had moved to live in the capital. So, even though we shared the... building... and genes, we weren't really close."

She could only remember a few times she'd gone over to her uncle's and it was never a particularly good memory. Tension seeped from the two estranged brothers to their children; a thorny wall between Doris and her cousins, more effective than the one made of bricks. She could see them in the street, knew they were just on the other side, but the gap was too wide and yawning.

"Nineteen years. Gods, this feels..." Doris didn't know how to finish the sentence. Bile clogged at her throat, constricting the airways. Why was there a pang, piercing through her lungs, deflating her? She hadn't even particularly liked her relatives.

So why was there now a crushing sorrow on her shoulders, just from looking at the beige furniture that didn't fit her memories? Of course things have changed. Even if her uncle or cousins were alive, they would've rearranged things, remodel, and replace the old with the new.

It was all a moot point. The dusty air and the lack of personal things were a sign of a dead hearth.

"In nineteen years, I've visited this cursed town only three times. For three funerals," she said, following an internal train of thought. She was only barely aware of Erika at her back, the stability and strength of her wife rooting her to the present. Otherwise, the past would've already dragged her down. "Covid, cancer, manslaughter," she counted, mostly for herself, since this wasn't new information to Erika. Out of the three, Doris was only truly grieving the last one. Her cousin Dorian was the kindest of that part of her extended family, always collecting stray dogs, giving them shelter. He had also been the first to die, the youngest. An experienced diver, he'd gone on a diving trip near a popular tourist destination and ended up caught in a speedboat's propellers at the hands of a drunk Brit joyriding over the sign for divers.

The dogs had ended up on the streets again after that.

The only funeral she'd missed was the last one, her uncle's, six years ago, stuck in the US at the time, as her father had reminded her, during the brutal coastal storms and subsequent flooding that threatened to devour New York City. Back then, trying to get out, Doris had figured that she was slowly witnessing the destruction of the whole branch of her family tree, and believed, for a moment, that she would be next.

She had been wrong.

"And now this."

A soft touch on her shoulder jolted her from morose thoughts. Erika's voice was close to her ear, warm breath tickling her naked skin. "Come, we should shower and make our bed. Whatever is to happen... we're in this together. You don't have to go through this alone."

Doris nodded, her eyes dry and filled with sand. She was being foolish, needlessly sad. This was all just the distant past to her anyway.

But not even the clear cold water, cleaning away the grease and the long hours on the road, could chase away the melancholy that had settled on her as soon as the red door opened.

Warmth cuddled her body—Erika snuggled close to Doris' chest, her deep breaths a soothing balm. Doris was aware of Erika's naked frame radiating heat, mingling with the staleness of the abandoned old house, even with operational air-conditioning blowing cool air. Erika had surrendered to peaceful sleep, but Doris, no matter how tired, couldn't do the same.

All the talk about wells had chipped away at her carefully constructed mind barriers keeping the memories at bay. It was the only reason she was able to fall asleep in a dark room, the only way she could stay sane each time she entered tunnels, or even her home at night before opening the lights.

Now, she was acutely aware of the darkness enveloping her from all sides, flooding her senses. Creeping over her naked skin with weightless fingers. A memory came to her, of a pitch-black nothingness, when she floated in the blank space, senseless and bodiless. She was transported to that moment where she ceased to exist, when her mind was reduced to a faint line of consciousness. Aware only of the infinite void, how it consumed her. She had wanted to scream but didn't have a mouth. Wanted to scratch the itch in her brain, but didn't have any arms or fingers or nails. She had wanted so desperately to open her eyes, but her eyelids were just one ingredient of the soup, just like the rest of her.

In the present, Doris opened her eyes, pushing out her suffocating memories, but the darkness of the room was not much better than the one conjured by her mind. Phantom pinpricks ghosted over her limbs, a paralyzing fear blanketing them. Erika's weight on Doris' chest was suddenly unbearable. That night, when she was just a brain floating in vacuum, the first sense of her body that she got back was being constricted by something around her, slimy, wet, and pulsating. Of her lungs unable to breathe in the warm liquid, screaming for air. She had to punch and scratch through this membrane wall until she broke out, head first, covered in blood and mucus.

Don't think about that, she said to her brain, but it only made her think even more about that night, replaying her emergence from the cocoon on a loop. Her father had later said she'd screamed, that it was what made him run towards her, but she hadn't really remembered much afterward, mostly staying in shock. She knew, intellectually, that he'd helped her get clean and drink some water, got her into her bed, but everything was a haze until the morning, when she fully got back to her senses. By the time she'd gone down the stairs on wobbly legs, her father had already taken care of the cocoon and was on his knees rubbing out the blood from the carpet. Her mother had already been in Rijeka, searching for a place for the two of them to live, and explaining to her what had happened was as weird as it could get, though mother couldn't ignore the truth in front of her eyes. Doris' metamorphosis was not something she would've been able to hide from her parents, even the one that didn't find her covered in bodily fluids.

With deep breaths, Doris forced her body to move, slowly untangling herself from her wife. Erika snorted and turned over to the other side, giving her much-needed space. Doris turned too, towards the nightstand, searching for her phone. The faint blue light dispersed the oppressive dark.

Carefully, quietly so as not to wake up Erika, she scrolled on her phone. Going through her short hair with one hand, she kept opening apps at random with the other one, just so she could have something else on her mind. She needed a distraction, some ridiculous online outrage, or short videos of pets, or anything, just not that nothingness at her back. There were a few messages from work—even when she was on vacation, she was getting urgent texts concerning bad reviews over Ariel's performance, the AI audiobook narrating software that she was working on. Something had glitched and the synthetic voice was mispronouncing some words, reading with the wrong emotions. Happy, when the character should've been sad and vice versa. Ended up with Ariel—the artificial narrator whose voice was modeled after a recently deceased, beloved actress—sounding like a bumbling sociopath, one of the beta readers apparently said. Doris rolled her eyes, but the annoyance over her job contacting her on her time off was at least a better emotion than this frightened state she'd found herself in. She needed a distraction, but not like this. Her team should find a way to deal with it without her help.

An image of a clear turquoise sea, calm and glistening in the sun, somewhere far, far away from her, showed up on her timeline. It mocked her. Agitated, she put the phone back on the nightstand but it only meant the room was plunged into the dark without its light.

The acid in her stomach roiled, and she got up from the bed, feeling around for her clothes. Acutely aware of any rustling noises she made, waiting with her breath held to see if Erika would turn, ask her what was wrong, why was she out of the bed. Was she dressing up? Where was she going?

Erika didn't turn, didn't wake up. She was fast asleep, lost in her dreams, unaware of her wife's spiking anxiety.

With soundless steps, Doris slipped away from the room, then out of the house on the street illuminated with silver moonlight and a glowing red haze from the direction of the sea.

"What the...?" The question slipped through her lips, fast and instinctive, too loud in a soundless night. Red illuminated the sky above the roofs and her legs moved, her eyes transfixed with the view.

Doris walked between the silent houses—leaning black masses crowding her—going down the slope. The dim yellows of the street lights barely shined at her path; consumed by the crimson and turned into a dreamy orange hue. She'd never experienced reality tinged like this, as if she were walking with a filter pulled over her eyes. Maybe she had fallen asleep. Her eyelids were a heavy weight, wanting to close down like shutters in her face, while her legs carried on almost of their own accord.

Shadows were deep and in motion, following her steps. A sensation of being watched burned at the nape of her neck. This was a mistake, a voice chided inside her head, *you should've stayed in the house, maybe moved to the living room and let the TV drain all possibility of nightmares from your brain.*

This should've worked too, a little stroll around a comatose town. She needed to move, to walk, to outrun her thoughts. And she wanted to know what was shining that bright crimson light. Her father hadn't mentioned this. He was right about the smell, though. It crawled up her nose, taking root inside her brain with its rot.

Outlined with scarlet lines, the ruins of the 14th-century fortress of some old Croatian Dukes—the Fortica—lay before her, behind the path overgrown with grass and thorns. It had seen a lot of battles, been rebuilt many times, but was now only an open wound, without a roof, its crumbling walls covered in moss. And something else, she suddenly remembered, halting her steps. The only thing that stood in the Fortica—an old well.

She used to go there during autumns and winters, when she was sure that the overgrown grass along the path to the fortress didn't hide any snakes. She would listen to the thunks of the chunks of the wall falling down and hitting the dry bottom. That had been *that* that night, while she was still a curious child who thought something good could crawl out of an abandoned well. Her palms itched with a memory of phantom pain—from the time she grasped at the walls, splitting open the skin on her hands, trying to climb out from the bottom of another well, one more ancient and impossible than this one standing here. She knew better now, and even though she could not see the well, she knew it was there, gaping open, waiting for her to fall down, again.

Not this time, she promised.

There was a hiss in the darkness of the fortress, accompanying a pair of reflecting green eyes. On top of the stairs leading to the well, a cat had crawled out from the shadows, warning Doris not to come near. It wasn't alone, she saw with goosebumps breaking all over, with more glowing eyes and dark shapes popping all over the fortress wall, seemingly countless, showing teeth, and with their fur electrified. Angry.

A bush in front of her rustled with movement and for a moment Doris could imagine hundreds of ravenous felines pounding at her, tearing at her meat with hungry mouths, lapping at her blood with spiny tongues. She rushed further down the path, wanting to leave it all behind—the wild cats and the open well inside the ruined fortress, before she learned how sharp the claws can get or how loud of a noise her body can make when it hits the dry ground.

Doris continued towards the sea, the tinge of red became brighter and more pronounced the closer she came to the shore. The wreckage of an 18th Century church stood against a background of a glowing red, the remaining tall walls and a belltower highlighted in crimson with the graveyard bathed in the same light. It had been bombed in the war, a long time ago, and the church was left like that, cleaved in half, for the Magistrala road to have enough space to pass through Karlobag. On the other side of the road was a beach, glistening with pearly red light. And the sea.

Which was a burning pool of blood.

Doris crossed the road, continued towards the water, coming to the end of a paved pier, and only then did she stop walking. She leaned over, her breathing shallow, yet it was impossible not to breathe in the foul stink of decaying flesh, decomposing vegetables, and rotten eggs. The surface was covered in luminus red slime, glowing brightly in the night. It stretched far, too far, towards Pag, blinding her. It washed her body in crimson, and even the sky was rusted red instead of a dark navy blue.

The slime bobbed on the surface of the resting sea and she had a ridiculous urge to kneel and touch it.

She wanted to know how it felt under her fingers. The texture it had. Did it burn?

What would happen if she jumped in the midst of it? She only needed to move another step, let the sea take her. It wouldn't be like old times, when her body used to slip through the clear cold water, refreshing her. No, she could imagine it like falling into the dense filth of a clogged sink, could feel the viscous muck clinging to her skin. Or, maybe, the slime was only floating on the surface, and the depths were clear of any residue? Maybe, under this pungent smell and bioluminescence, the same old murky blue sea she remembered lay awaiting her? She only needed to take one step further, and she would know.

A surge of warm breath tickled her neck for just a second before she whirled around so fast she almost lost her balance and truly fell into the sea behind. Blood rushed to her ears, pumped by a fast-beating heart. The crimson burned brightly in her eyes and icy sweat broke all over her.

There was no one behind her, only the serpentine road and the church ruin doused with the crimson light. She put her hand over her chest, feeling the quick rhythm of a drum. A movement at her feet grabbed her attention and her eyes fell down. Painted in the glowing red, a dark, elongated body slithered on the pier. A triangle-shaped head, with reflecting yellow eyes, firmly fixed on Doris.

Dread of another kind replaced her earlier fear. "You're only a snake," she whispered. It was summer. There were snakes everywhere, hiding under the rocks, in the bushes, or just sunbathing on the road. *It was only a snake*, she wanted to say again but the words caught in her throat. Cold rushed in her veins, flowing with her blood.

The snake swirled before her eyes in hypnotizing patterns. In the background, a foggy mist started seeping from the mountain, rolling out over the town, obscuring the church right before her. Faintly, Doris was aware of the clean air of the mountain top and the undulating rock formations sticking towards the sky, razor-sharp.

Some hidden reflex—locked in the heart of a bird caged in her lungs—kicked in and she firmly closed her eyes.

"Please, not again. No," she said, even when she knew it was futile. What were her wishes to the powers older than the first settlement from which the town had grown like a tumor, older than the islands of the Adriatic Sea? She was only a small speck of sentient dust, stuck in the eyes of the great unknown.

The mist slid over her body with grabbing cold hands, twisting her insides like a wet washing cloth. Her body went through a sensation not unlike the moment when an airplane takes off—that sense of losing connection to gravity, like it was cut out with a clean strike; getting ripped from the land and hurled into the skies. Her mind screamed in the animalistic shriek of a mammal not made for flight, but her mouth stayed closed shut. It was an effort that left her with a bruised jaw and bitten tongue, the metallic taste filling her mouth. She was aware of her arms closed around her chest, hugging her in a tight grip. Her legs were an iron weight, paralysed in dread.

And then it all stopped as fast as it had overcome her, the mist spitting her out, her feet reconnecting with the solid ground. The shock of it threw off her balance and she dropped like a log, falling on a sharp, protruding rocky surface, with her hands outstretched. The stinging pain burned through her palms, forcing her to open her eyes.

The rock stopped her from tumbling down the slope, which was only a faint outline drawn in darkness. Blood slowly trickled from the shredded skin on her arms. When she raised her palm, she saw a red smear left where she'd split it open on stone. The blood dissipated before her eyes as the mountain drank it. Would that be enough, or would it ask for more? She felt another rock pressing at her back. She was put between two fingers, no, two teeth of the mountain's jaws, as if she were a food stuck between; not a comparison she wanted to entertain. The snake was curling close to her legs, flicking its forked tongue.

First things first, Doris thought, taking in a deep breath, calming herself. Her rigid body slowly let out the tension from her limbs. First, she became aware of the cooling air chilling the sweat on her skin. She shivered, not dressed enough for high altitude, in her shorts and shirt. But she was alive, at the place that was opposite of the tight space of the well and, even wedged between two rocks, she didn't feel so constricted, since it was what had kept her from falling down.

Then she raised her head and the sight punched out the remaining air from her lungs.

The far-outstretching sea of the Velebit channel was a red, simmering bruise separating the mainland from the huge, bare body of the island of Pag. The crimson hands were grabbing towards the island's shore and it felt like only a matter of time before they caught up to it. She was reminded of the gray growth on her father's bold head, advancing over the pink flesh. The same way was the red trying to cover the entirety of the canal.

But she was outside of it, high up the mountain, where the air was crisp and clear, and the night was illuminated by a silvery moonlight, rather than the fires of hell.

"It's growing." Words whispered as if carried on the wind. A memory of the bora rushing down the mountain and slamming at the window shutters of her childhood room sounded in her ears. "At first it was only a small circle of red around the dock, a blooming cherry."

"Why am I here?" Doris asked, her lips finally ungluing. She was shaking uncontrollably, and it wasn't only from the cold of the mountain air. The chill she felt went deeper than that. She wasn't even certain whom she was asking. The snake that was slithering over her legs? Velebit? The god or the mountain?

Whichever force had taken her the first time, nineteen years ago, and toyed with her for whatever reason.

"Don't play games with me," she bit out, her eyes moving away from the red towards her immediate surroundings. She was on a neck-breaking slope which was only a black mass in the night, that much she knew. Branches of a short tree were visible under the moonlight on her left, close enough to scratch her if she leaned closer. Since she could see the Velebit channel, she was still on Northern Velebit, above Karlobag, which meant a lot of underbrush and trees that she couldn't see, but knew were covering the slope before her.

But on her right, at some distance, she saw the outline of something slim, pointing towards the channel and, even beyond that, the shape of something circular with a black cube behind it. She understood then where she was. The first shape was a telescope, mounted for a better view. The second and the third ones were old stone monuments erected on these spots to commemorate the building of roads over the mountain. It was *the* place for tourists who wanted to see the view extending over the sea, Pag, and the entire Velebit channel. Easily accessible from the road, they didn't even need to climb to get to it.

This was not the ninth well. But if the snake was the same one that had kept her captive in the well, what was it doing here? Why did it bring Doris here with it? To see the channel?

To see the red consuming it.

"Your world is done." The voiceless words floated over on her neck to her ear, smelling of springtime and hawthorn. They were not in her head but spoken through the winds of time. "We have seen so many changes. From the islands forming, to the first huts rising over our bones, turning then to stone to bricks to roads to wars." The last part wasn't spoken so much as shown to her, a glimpse of memory so old it hurt her brain to process all that information. She couldn't think about it, didn't want to focus on the images Velebit was trying to show her, fearing it would clear out all of the space in her memory, only to replace it with a smidgen of forbidden knowledge.

"And now there's something new, so what?" she gritted through her teeth, a headache blooming under the pressure of trying to make sense of this conversation.

The triangle head of the snake by her legs waved left and right.

"This is something... unlike everything before. It's coming here... to us. It broke through your world to the world of our dreams."

"Let me repeat my question: so what," she said, her blood pumping faster, anger waking up inside her. She was shivering in the cold, ripped out from her place without being asked first, thrown around like a rubber boat in a storm. "Are you envious because something is so weird and so new you can't understand it? It's beyond your comprehension and as such beyond your control?" She giggled, desperately. "This is how we humans feel all the time, especially when something ancient and powerful takes us out to play with." Her words were bitter poison, and a part of her felt fear for antagonizing the thing that held her in its grasp. "Why do you even care? You'll be fine."

"Nothing is fine," the mountain grumbled under her feet, shaking as if awakened by an earthquake. "No one will be fine. This is not the natural order of events. This is the end."

The snake's head pointed at the glowing sea. The surge of visions clouded over her eyes—of a swollen sea rising high, climbing the mountain, devouring the land, until nothing but a small peak remained as a lonely island.

"You successfully killed your world, and this time, you're dragging us with you to this destruction."

The accusation was as sharp as the rock that kept digging in her back. Bubbling from within came the things her father used to say to her, over and over—while she still bothered to communicate with him; all of the blame he put on her because of the job she did. As if she were personally guilty for all the terrible things that happened in the world, as if she were the one who wrote the laws, or was in charge of the corporation she worked at. He always managed to throw the guilt into her face. Making her feel like some voice-snatching witch just because she worked at helping publishing churn out audiobooks faster and cheaper. As if she'd betrayed everything he'd taught her, every single storyteller she'd seen perform as a child when he took her with him on his research trips. If they hadn't fought over her insistence on turning her back to Karlobag and Velebit, it was over that. But, in a way, it was all the same fight. In his eyes, the mountain had gifted her something magical, and she'd walked all over it to go work for a soulless company which produced more soulless things. And, as the worst offense, she kept the story of that night for herself. She never told him the full tale, never wanted to share it with the rest of the world. Doris even forbade him to write about it.

This version of the ninth well was hers, and only hers, a fact that her father could never accept.

Her stomach roiled, frustrations twisting it in a knot.

"Everything needs to die, sooner or later," she burst out, anger dripping from her words. "You think it doesn't apply to you? Why wouldn't it? Death is the one constant, one certainty of life. You just aren't used to the feeling of your own mortality." She was laughing now, and couldn't believe herself. Shouting angrily at a god—if Erika was correct in calling it that. "I don't understand what I have to do with that. Do you think I'm personally responsible for you?"

The snake shook its head, and even though it didn't have a face, Doris could see it was dissatisfied. Just like her father. She lived to disappoint. Fathers or ancient powers beyond her comprehension; it was all the same.

Tears swelled in her eyes, and if she started crying now, it would turn into an avalanche that would not stop. The ugly laugh and the tears would drown the town sleeping below.

If Erika were here, she would've shown respect. She would've listened to what the ancient one had to say. And she definitely wouldn't have told it to accept it will die in the end, just like everybody else. Erika, who was sleeping peacefully in bed, ignorant of what was happening to her wife. Why couldn't have Doris just fallen asleep at her side and skipped this nonsense?

Doris wasn't her wife, though. She was tired of her father's disappointment, of the world going to shit, of the knowledge that there were powers that could change so much, help so many people, but who were largely callous, or simply following their own incomprehensible design. Why could she get her heart's desires, while the original tale of the well with the hidden treasures came from people who went to sleep with empty bellies, dreaming of gold that could save them from poverty? "Do you think I can do something about the sea?" If that was the case, the gods were even more delusional than her father. "Why am I here?" she added, frustrated, shaking so hard from anger that she didn't even feel the cold anymore. "Why did you steal me away?" A horrifying thought broke through her brain, lighting panic under her feet. *Will you let me back?*

But the wind stayed silent and the snake kept watching her intently, its head high on its neck, the body coiled under it. The mountain shook in disgust. Somewhere far away, and yet close, in the realm just a breath away behind her back, was a deep dark well.

If she concentrated on it, she could see that empty, hungry hole.

Doris shook her head, trying to clear her mind from the memories. From the calling she felt.

"Just, will you let me go back? Please? I just want to go to sleep." She hated to be reduced to begging. But the fear of getting stuck in the well, forever stolen away from Erika and her life, to be stashed away like a shiny gem, was all too real. If she had to plead to get back, she'll prostrate herself before the old gods, no matter her rage and indignation.

The snake flickered its forked tongue and blinked out of existence as if it were never there. The mountain calmed, satiated on her blood, already uncaring. As if it had forgotten that she even existed after doing to her whatever it wanted to. The cold air hugged her, seeping through the warm layer of anger and fear.

She was completely alone high up on the mountain, without a car to get back to the town below, or a phone to call her wife. Abandoned to the cold and despair, with palms painfully shredded. Wearing cheap flip-flops that could easily twist under her feet, making her tumble down the slope she'd been placed upon before she could even get to the road.

Her furious scream broke through the night, rolling over the hills like the northern wind.

CHAPTER 3

"WHAT THE FUCK, YOU fucking asshole!" Doris yelled at the empty stone mass rising all around her. By car, it was a twenty minutes drive from this spot to Karlobag, but she had no idea how long it would take her on foot. The road was a serpentine drop and she was pretty certain the walk would last for hours. Not to mention she wasn't in shape as she once was, when she used to hike with her father regularly. She couldn't remember the last time she'd walked for more than thirty minutes. At least it was all downhill.

There were two things she could do. Extract herself from the two rocks she'd found herself between and find a way to the path; from there she just had to follow it towards the monuments. The last one, the cube-like one, was literally connected to the road with a short flight of stairs, so she had to get to it and that's the hardest part done. After that she needed to follow the road—there were scattered vacation houses and a village close by down the mountain, so she might find people there. She could go in the opposite direction, too, towards the hostel that was popular with hikers, but she wasn't sure if it was still open. Just like she wasn't sure that the village on the mountain wasn't abandoned. The village was in the right direction, at least, no need to make her trip longer if it turns out that the hostel was long closed.

Or—the third option—she could stay, cry, shout and freeze till morning, hoping someone would find her in time. How would Erika or her father even locate her? They wouldn't even think to look up the mountain. They would look for her in town, call the police, maybe search the sea thinking that she'd lost her mind and gone for a nice nighttime swim, and it would be forever before they came up here.

There was a chance that someone might pass by the road. The town was a black hole for tourism, but this was not Karlobag. Her chances would definitely be better on the road.

Firstly, the flip-flops problem. They were flat and light, easy to twist on uneven rocks if she made just one wrong move, and if that happened, she could see her leg twisting with them. The best-case scenario would be a swollen ankle, the worst an open skull, her brain splattered over the stones. But the alternative would be to walk on the underbrush and stone on bare feet, risking her skin to the needle-pointed edges in the dark. Not to mention possible crawlies. Which one was worse?

A nervous laugh bubbled out of her while she removed them from her feet. To die on Velebit with flip-flops on would be the most humiliating way to go for a local to the mountain. She remembered that tourists used to die this way in summer, going hiking completely unprepared for the terrain. Thinking that Velebit was a tame park where they could run away from the heat a bit on a nice little stroll. They would walk in their sandals, get lost, dehydrate, and the mountain would gorge on their sacrifice. Doris' father used to say that you knew that the summer season had started in earnest when you heard the first tourist died. And that's the man who planned on renting out an apartment.

The stone under the soft soles of her feet was rough, the low grass sharp as nails. It was like walking on shards of glass. Behind her spot, a slight stone formation created a short wall she had to pass to get to the other side, the safe side. Feeling her way with her feet, to be sure of the rock's balance and stability—checking each stone and skipping over those that shook under her soles, threatening to fall over—she slowly stepped onward.

Stepping over like that, half-blind in the night, she managed to climb down from the ridge to the path. For one, dizzying moment she stayed standing like that, legs shaking. At least the mountain hadn't put her on the top of some peak and left her there to find a way to hike down. This was doable, almost a normal stroll someone might take on their vacation, albeit during the day. Not that it meant she wasn't pissed at being put in this situation in the first place. This was why she never believed in the specialness her father tried to make her out to have. She wasn't some chosen one, a divine child or whatever. If she were blessed or in any special position, the mountain wouldn't act like she was a plastic bag of chips to be thrown away once it was finished eating.

With a loud groan, she put back her flip-flops and started walking toward the telescope. This was the hand-made marble path, clean of grass and dangerous rocks. Narrow, but easy to follow. She still advanced slowly, careful how she walked and each step she took, not wanting to do a wrong thing and stumble and fall.

At least the monuments were close enough. She passed the telescope that had to be all rusted over now, the circular rock bench with a round stone table in the middle, the monument resembling a broken tooth, its carved words long turned unreadable by the weather and time, and in the end the Kubus—a cube placed on four spheres, celebrating the building of the road connecting Karlobag and the town on the other side of the mountain.

It was only then, when she was already at the cube, that she could see not only the road below but also the old shack she'd forgotten even existed. And a thing that made her gasp and laugh out in surprise.

A van, as dark as the night around her, was parked in front of the shack.

Unthinking, she rushed down the stone stairs to the road, and crashed at the doors of the shack as fast and loud as the bora, banging at it with her aching palms.

"Is there anyone here!? Hello!" Through the cracks between the boards, she could see a faint blue light. Muffled sounds of scratching and hushed voices were the sweetest melody she could wish for and she giggled in euphoria. There was someone on the other side of the doors. She wasn't alone. She didn't need to worry about whether the village downhill was still populated, if there was anyone vacationing in one of the mountain houses. Whether she'd have to walk for hours.

But the doors stayed closed, even when she could easily discern footsteps and whispers, locating multiple someones on the other side. It dawned on her, at that moment, that she probably didn't sound like the most harmless person, showing up in the middle of the night literally out of nowhere and banging at the door like a demon from hell. She noticed a warm, wet smear on the door where she'd hit with her stinging palms, almost as if marking it.

Calming herself down with deep breaths, she tried to sound more innocent and less ax-wielding slasher. "Please, I need help. I'm stuck here, I need to get off the mountain. Please!"

She let just a bit of a panic tinge her tone, modulating it with enough vulnerability to leave an impression of someone harmless and in need of help. It did the trick, and the doors opened, letting the low light from computer monitors break out.

Highlighted by this bluish hue, a woman with a sidecut, a bit shorter than Doris, gripped the door, clearly frightened. Behind the woman stood a tall, willowy man with a high afro puff. He held something long and sharp in his hand, ending in prongs and buzzing with electricity, pointed toward Doris. It was at that moment that Doris' brain finally caught up with the fact that this shack was a minuscule, single room with a roof, and not a vacation house, and that, the same way they had no idea what Doris was doing there in the middle of the night, it was also true in reverse.

Doris raised her arms, palms open, showing that she had no intention of hurting either of them, wondering whether she should be concerned for her own safety. There was a whole lot of tech inside and something... similar to an aquarium, on the table, but the man shifted, blocking the view inside the shack.

"We... we, er, don't understand Croatian. Do you speak English? Are you in trouble?" the woman asked her in English, with a New York accent.

"I speak fluent English, German, Italian and French, and a bit of Hungarian and Russian. What about you?" Doris answered, annoyed. It was a normal question to ask, since she came to them speaking Croatian, but she still felt slighted. As if she were some backwater hick. Especially since it was a normal thing for Croatians to speak at least one more language—Italian if they were living on the west coast, German if they were living in the north, and English as a default, especially for those who lived and worked in the tourist spots. Not counting the other Slavic languages that were similar enough to understand them naturally.

Well, she was in the middle of nowhere. She had to relax, stop assuming they were trying to insult her, and try not to sound like a douche if she wanted help from these people.

"Are you in some kind of trouble?" The woman repeated, ignoring her jab, searching her face with dark eyes behind big, round glasses, and glimpsing behind Doris's back. "How did you get here? We didn't hear any vehicles..." she trailed off, as if uncertain. With a movement of her head, Doris noticed a tattoo on the woman's neck, a splatter of color, not easily identifiable in this light. She appeared to be of Asian descent, but Doris couldn't say more than that. She wasn't good with facial features, her job was with voices and spoken sounds.

"But we did hear... I told you it was a *human* scream," the woman's companion hissed, in a slight British accent, low, but clear enough for Doris to hear. His hand with a prong-like thing was shaking a bit, the sounds of electricity sparkling.

She could hear the quiet whirring of computers, but nothing else from the inside.

"Was that you?" the woman asked, concerned. "I thought it was some kind of animal, for sure. Are you alright? Are you hurt?" She finally moved from the doors, looking for something in her pockets. When she drew out her phone and opened the torch app, Doris had to shield her eyes from the blinding white light. "Oh my... what happened to your palm? Did you *fall* down the hill?"

"Can you please stop beaming the light right into my fucking eyes? Thank you."

The woman apologized, pointing it down at their legs. She seemed young, well, younger than Doris, maybe in her late twenties or early thirties, but Doris wouldn't bet on her assessment.

"Look, I'm sort of stuck here. Could you lend me your phone to make one quick call? I just want to call my wife to come pick me up."

"How did you even get here?" the man asked, lowering the hand with the pointy stick, probably deciding she wasn't a threat.

"That's not important. Please. I need to go back to Karlobag and I would rather do that by car. The walk could take hours."

"Oh! Well, in that case, we could drop you off," the woman proposed.

The man let out an undignified gasp. "Chloe," he hissed towards her, clearly not impressed.

"What? We were talking about wrapping up here anyway." The woman—Chloe, apparently—smiled at Doris. "If all you need is to get down there, give us a few minutes and we'll drive you. We're also staying in the town."

"Are you certain you wouldn't rather I called for help?" Doris asked, her brain already sifting through the possible dangers she could put herself in by accepting. She didn't know a thing about who these two were or what they were doing. But she also depended on their help, and that would've been true for anyone she found along the road on the way down.

"It's not a problem if you want to call your wife so she doesn't worry, but as I said, we were ready to get back anyway. Why make her drive here?"

Doris looked long and hard at both of them, the open face of a woman who was clearly curious about Doris' sudden appearance, and the man's obvious concern. He didn't look too happy with the idea of them picking up a stranger, which she couldn't fault him for. It made her more inclined to accept the offer. If he was worried she was a murderous creep, that meant he wasn't one.

Erika was probably still sound asleep and would need to dress up first and get to the car, and every minute longer was a minute Doris didn't need to wait if she took the foreigners up on their offer.

"Fine," she said and Chloe beamed while the man looked constipated. Probably suppressing the need to groan.

The drive to town was pregnant with curiosity, tangible in the air among them. Chloe was constantly throwing sideway looks at her while she drove, obviously wanting to know what had happened to Doris. On the other hand, Doris was burdened with a growing interest herself. Chloe and Tendai—which is how the man introduced himself before they got in the car—had in the van various equipment, cameras, computers, even drones, as well as something she was fairly certain was an underwater cage and more stuff she didn't recognize. What were they doing up on Velebit in the middle of the night, with all of that? At least it wasn't duct tapes and ropes.

And they were *American*. Well, Chloe was, at least, but Tendai's British accent meant nothing; he could, like Doris, live and work away from his homeland. Doris remembered, briefly, the comment she'd made to her father. Were they the researchers her mother had mentioned? But wouldn't they be working on samples in a lab somewhere?

Squeezed in the front bench seat between Chloe and Tendai, she drummed her fingers on her knee, thinking about how to broach the subject, without it being used as an excuse to probe back into her business.

"So... I'm guessing you guys aren't tourists. Because if you are, someone ripped you off."

Chloe laughed. "The place we rent is actually super cheap. And we're almost on the beach. Well, close enough. I'm pretty sure there's no way you would get any sort of place for that money, anywhere else."

"No, but it's all about what's your goal. If you're here for some vacation time, to sunbathe and swim a bit, it doesn't matter how cheap the accommodations are. You're still not going to have a good time."

"I wouldn't say that. I'm having a great time," Chloe joked, her lips stretched in an amused smile.

"You're the only one," Tendai said from Doris' right. "This town is depressing as hell... with what happened to it."

"It was depressing even before all this," Doris acknowledged.

"You're local?" Chloe asked, her eyes now firmly on the serpentine road, but Doris would bet it didn't have to do with being careful as much as giving an appearance of not being as interested in the question. "Or are you into disaster tourism?"

"I used to be. Local, I mean. Currently, I'm in Ireland, though I've lived for a bit in New York," she conceded. It wasn't a secret. The only thing she didn't want to discuss was her appearing on the mountain. She was too tired to think of a plausible explanation for that. "I came to see my dying father. The sea is killing him."

Tendai flinched at her words, so hard she felt it, sitting next to him. Chloe's face fell, and she turned towards Doris for a second before looking back towards the road. "Oh, shit, I'm sorry. I didn't mean to joke..."

"You did. But that's okay." She wasn't interested in apologies. She wanted to know what these people were doing here. But if they were here to research the bacteria, they were probably under some kind of NDA, because they hadn't offered any sort of information on their work. She assumed it wouldn't be such a problem to mention they were researchers otherwise.

They drove the rest of the trip downhill in choking silence, and their guilt was so palpable Doris almost wanted to force the issue, bursting with curiosity. But she was too tired and wanted nothing more than to return to her wife and her former home.

Chloe parked in the same parking lot Doris had, and she could see her car where she'd left it, highlighted by the glowing red bioluminescence, making her remember seeing a black van parked there. It was the same one she was sitting in right now.

"Thank you. You saved me from a long trip downhill," Doris said, once outside, stretching her legs. She didn't need to fake gratitude. Chloe was shifting awkwardly, like she wasn't certain what to do with her arms, while Tendai hung by the rear doors.

"Don't mention it. I'm just glad we could help," Chloe said, with a small smile.

Tendai shrugged. "It was all Chloe. No offense, but up there, I wasn't ready to find myself in a folk horror story."

Doris couldn't help herself, she burst out laughing at that, leaving them chuckling behind.

"I couldn't find the ambulance you mentioned and the pharmacy looked like something out of a zombie apocalypse movie. I'm dead serious; the shelves are half-empty and dusty, *dusty*, as if they were looted weeks ago. No, not weeks, years," Erika started ranting as soon as she was back in the house, a tote bag hanging from her shoulder. The faint industrial smell of sunscreen wafted in with her. It was early in the morning, but she'd still made sure to cover herself in a gracious layer before braving the sun's radiation.

Doris groaned from her space on the couch, rubbing sleep from her eyelids. She had managed to doze off on the couch, waiting for Erika to come back from the shopping trip, which wasn't that surprising, given how she'd only managed to catch a few hours of sleep during the night. After stumbling into a very awake and very worried Erika, who was ready to take off to the strange town alone and mount a search for her foolish wife who'd left during the night, without her phone or a message about where she'd gone to.

The wounds on Doris' palms had hurt, but it had been nothing compared to Erika's disappointed look.

In the present, her wife dropped the bag on the table with a loud clunk. There was some residual anger in that movement, Doris guessed.

"I managed to get the bandages, but they didn't have any antiseptic."

"I don't think it's that serious, anyway." Doris waved her hand. She came to the table and Erika took her palms into her hands. Erika's soft fingers caressed the edges of the irritated pink flesh, where few strips of skin were missing. The red glinted in the morning light breaking through the open shutters.

"Let's at least get this cleaned and bandaged."

After Doris washed her hands in cold water, Erika helped her put white gauze on them before wrapping them in bandages.

"Did you have any problems in town? Did you see anyone?" Doris asked while Erika was working on her left palm.

Erika hummed and shrugged. "Only the pharmacist who looked at least a hundred years old. I think the sole reason why she isn't retired is that they don't have anyone to replace her." She clicked her tongue, looking at her work. It was clean and precise, with no band out of place, and she nodded approvingly before going back to the right hand. "Do you know what she told me?"

Oh, no, thought Doris, cringing internally in anticipation.

"She praised my Croatian."

Doris snorted a laugh, feeling second-hand embarrassment since it was the town she'd grown up in and, as such, it used to be her community. "What did you say to that?"

"I said something along the lines of, 'well, I should certainly hope, since it's my mother tongue'. At that, she was a bit confused, but then her brain probably caught up on what I said, so she started to apologize. And, get this, she said she thought I was one of the Americans who came to town last month. After all, there's a black man in the group, so it was an easy mistake to make." Erika rolled her eyes.

"Last month?"

"Yep." Erika closed the last bandage, turning her palm over and admiring her work. But the crooked smile that tugged on her lip indicated that she enjoyed teasing Doris with her gathered intel. Maybe she will make her work on getting it all out from her, as revenge for scaring her last night.

"And?" Doris asked through a dry mouth. She needed

to drink some water or, better yet, take another cup of coffee.

"The pharmacist is a bit of a nosy baba," Erika continued. "So, I'm sort of 'confused' how she could've mixed me with them, but whatever, moving on to more interesting stuff. At least she didn't ask me if I was adopted.

"Anyway, it appears there's four of them and they've rented out a house and a couple of boats. The townsfolk—though I'm not sure how many that includes because, again, all of the houses are closed down and there was no one outside—keep seeing them out at sea. They're not really upfront about what they're doing, but it's clear they're conducting some kind of experiments. They even *dive*, and have a drone that's doing daily flyovers. Too loud, says the pharmacist. A lot of times it wakes her up or she can't get to sleep because of it at night. But that's not the most interesting part."

Erika stopped at that for a dramatic pause, not dissimilar to the storytellers of old. Her brown eyes twinkled with a conspiratorial gleam. Doris was at the edge of her seat, waiting with a raised eyebrow.

"Guess whom they spoke with. Or tried too, at least."

If her eyebrow could climb to the edge of her hairline, it probably would. "No, don't tell me—"

"Yes, exactly. Everyone knows they had sought out the local grumpy old man who promptly threw them out of his house."

Doris sighed and closed her eyes, pinching the bridge of her nose.

"That's one interesting tidbit, but there's another very intriguing one. Or at least that's how the pharmacist presented it." At this, Erika sobered up. "I mean, it's idle gossip, so who knows what exactly happened." She shrugged, but Doris knew she was only feigning being casual. Doris knew every sound her wife's voice made and what each of them meant. "There used to be five of them in the beginning. One day, there were only four. And one of the boats they'd rented was found out at sea. Abandoned... and bloody." She let the sentence trail off, let it sink in. "At least, that's what the pharmacist told me. Of course, you could always ask yourself how the fuck she knows that. Or you could just accept it at face value."

Doris frowned. A mysterious group doing shady stuff, a missing person, with possible foul play, and, in the middle of that, her darling father. "Let's go see what my dad has to say about all this. I will kill him myself if it turns out he rejected people who might've helped him, and dragged me here instead, with some nebulous ideas of magical healing."

"Well, to be honest," Erika started, and Doris knew right away she would hate whatever came next. "You were here only for one night before a powerful, *magical* being whisked you away on an adventure. So, you could say that he wasn't exactly wrong." She was teasing, but there was some truth in what she said, and Doris hated that.

"Too bad I pissed it off before getting a chance to ask it to heal my father, nicely," she said with a sigh. "Maybe it's better not to mention to father my last night's—how did you put it—adventures." The knowledge that she'd had the chance to plead his case to the higher being and completely failed to do it, choosing to get into a fight with it instead, could both break him and toughen his resolve that he was right in asking her to come back.

What if she's missed the only chance to actually do

something to make him better? To make the town better?

No. She wasn't the one with the power. If it wanted to help, it could, at any moment. But that didn't change the crushing weight of guilt she felt settling in her stomach instead of breakfast.

Stribor greeted them with a wagging tail completely covered in gray growth. She petted his coarse, light brown head, avoiding the patches of growing scales, a sickening feeling driving her hand.

The shutters were down and the windows shut, the living room illuminated only with the dim yellow light of a light bulb quickly losing its power. The air was heavy with the sweltering heat, drying out all the fluids in her body, bringing them out in droplets of sweat that made twin lakes under her armpits. But it was nothing compared to the decaying smell of fungi eating through yellow pages of books and the bacteria eating through the body of her father and his dog. It was even worse than yesterday. How could he withstand it?

Erika was walking between the stacks, her hand languidly passing the covers, face scrunched.

"Breakfast?" father asked, a large moka pot in his hand.

"That's okay, we're not hungry," Doris said. The mere idea of putting something in her mouth was enough for her to taste the vomit. Erika threw her a thankful look while absently leafing through a book.

"What happened to you?" father asked, pointing at Doris' hands.

"I went on a stroll last night, and fell in the dark. It's nothing big, just scratches." The omission didn't help with the nausea, the lie falling as heavy as spoiled food, poisoning her.

"You were out last night? On a stroll? In the doomed town? Was it fun?"

"And what about you?" she asked him instead. "Are you even allowed to drink coffee?"

"It's liquid." He shrugged. "Doris, I'm dying either way. The only reason why I don't stuff myself with regular food is that my stomach can't handle it and I throw it all up."

He poured all of it into a cup and sat down. The dog immediately went to him on his wobbly legs. It was a depressing sight that the two of them made—both riddled with clusters of gray scales, too thin, sick, and ancient.

"Mom didn't say you took in the dog. How old is he even?"

"He's somewhere between seventeen and eighteen years old, a lot for a dog," he said with a sigh and leaned over to pet him. Unlike Doris, her father didn't avoid the unnatural growth, petting all over his small head. "He was one of Dorian's dogs, one of his rescues. Do you remember them?" How could I not? she almost said but didn't get the chance to open her mouth before her father continued. "Your uncle threw them all out when Dorian died, but I kept this one. He was the ugliest of the pack. One of the oldest too, I knew he had no chance of getting adopted. No one would want him."

"Someone wanted him, though" Her wife's voice was kind and tone low. She went over to the couch to sit, but Doris had too much nervous energy to join her. She kept standing in the middle of the living room, arms crossed over her chest.

"He's a loyal dog. Misses Dorian even after all these

years. Dorian used to take him along when he was working on a tourist submarine boat, but the dog was too afraid of the boat, so he would wait for him on the dock. After Dorian's death, he would go to the docks every day, intently watching the sea, waiting for Dorian to come back, thinking he was just out working. I couldn't explain to him that Dorian was not coming back, so I let him do that. Now, though, he's too old and too deaf to walk around the town alone and I'm too old and weak to go with him."

The sudden urge to apologize to him was strong, but she wasn't sure what exactly she should be sorry for. Going with her mother after the divorce and leaving him behind? Not calling and checking on him for years because it was easier like that, when they didn't have to communicate? Forgetting about him last night? Or, simply, to express how hard it was for her to see him like this, knowing it will not be long before he joins his nephew six feet underground?

"So, I met interesting people last night. Some strangers. Do you know anything about them?" It was easier just to change the subject.

"I don't get out much, as I said before." His voice was flat, without emotion.

"Don't bullshit me, I know they tried to talk with you. What about?"

"Why did you act like you didn't know, then? Are you some sort of police now, playing mind games with your suspect?"

Doris gritted her teeth. "Don't be dramatic and answer me."

He pouted. Like some small child caught in trouble, not the old man that he was. Though, there's that saying that the older people get, the more they revert to their childhood days.

"They wanted to talk about what happened six years ago. What I remembered of that time when I noticed the first skin lesions, do I remember anything weird happening before that, stuff like that."

"Why? Did they say why they wanted to know that?" Erika popped into the conversation, curiosity lacing her tone.

Father's sigh was deep and profound as if they were asking him to solve the mysteries of the universe. The dog was under him, curled up on his feet, dozing off.

"They said they were from some American Institute, doing some research and something about me being patient zero. Though, honestly, I wasn't paying much attention, and I'm pretty sure there was someone else sick before me... I wasn't that interested in what they had to sell."

He put up his hand to stop Doris, probably anticipating her reaction. "Before you start shouting at me, take into account that I was in gut-searing pain when they came to my door. It was before I was put on a liquid diet and I'd spent most of the morning throwing up my guts. And I say this almost literally."

"That's... not possible," Erika whispered, clearly unsure if he was being hyperbolic or not.

"You could say, I wasn't in the mood," he concluded and sipped more coffee.

"And later? They've been here for a month, the town is small, you can't say you couldn't find out where they were and see what they wanted." Not to mention, she was fairly certain they'd left some kind of contact, unless he'd threatened someone with bodily harm and they decided he wasn't worth it.

"I know where they are," he said, nonchalant.

"They're renting out old Danica's house."

"You're joking."

"Why would I be?"

"Which house is that?" Erika interrupted them, watching Doris, who silently fumed.

"The neighbor's." The image of the strange man in the window, smoking cigarettes when they first came here, watching them, swam in her mind's eye. He was probably one of them. "And in all this time you haven't bothered talking with them? For fuck's sake, you could've talked from your window, and none of you would've even had to get out of your living rooms."

"Doris, I don't care about them," her father said, "and they don't care about me. It's mutual."

"How can you be so sure? You said it yourself, they're here from some Institute. Maybe they're trying to find a cure."

"If that were the truth, they wouldn't be on location, they would be in some fancy, high-tech laboratory somewhere. They would try to get me to that fancy laboratory and run all sorts of tests on me. They wouldn't waste their time out at sea. Maybe for a few samples, but not for a whole month. No, sweetheart, I'm not that interesting to them. They probably hoped that I'll have some information for them, but I doubt it would've been helpful for me."

The endearment must've fallen from his lips subconsciously, but it rang out in Doris' head, loud and clear. It didn't help that the last time he'd used it was the day she was packing, when he asked her to stay with him, rather than go with her mom.

To her angry teenage mind, it wasn't even a competition. Her mother was moving away to the big city, where Doris could easily disappear in the background, be just one of many, invisible, not someone everybody knew about and thought they had a right to her business. And for her mother, Doris didn't need to be something more, didn't need to be perfect; just herself.

But the memory of him standing at the door, his icy blue eyes watery, telling her *You can stay with me, sweetheart,* was now as fresh as her shredded palms. She'd managed to forget all about that, but now it resurfaced with a vengeance, clogging her throat.

"Well, even if their objective is something else, they're obviously conducting some sort of research," Erika said, and Doris was grateful for that, unsure she could unstick her dry mouth to say anything. "It could end up helping you. Scientists share information."

"If enough money is involved," he said with an exhausted sigh. "Look, I understand what you're saying. I do. But I don't share your optimism or your hope. We all remember the first pandemic, even the two of you, you weren't small enough to forget. Besides, I'm no one's lab rat. It's undignified."

"Why are you so stubborn?" Doris finally asked, through gritted teeth.

"I'm not. I just know how the world works. Our town, our small patch of the sea, it's unimportant. We don't move the economy. We don't have an oil rig, we aren't some important fishing site, nor a tourist spot. The only ones who remotely care if our bacteria spreads are the Pag islanders." He took deep, ragged breaths, on the verge of coughing. "In the beginning... it wasn't like that in the beginning. People came here, drawn by the news of a shiny new bacteria. Tons of media coverage, and scientists in big boats. Papers and papers written, interviews, news, conspiracy theories, and such. People came to take selfies with the red glimmer once the bioluminescence kicked in. Do you see anyone like that anymore? The worse the detritus got, the worse it started to smell, and the fewer people came. The uglier our skin lesions developed, the less entertaining we were. And since there was no money to be made here, we soon slipped from everyone's mind."

"Someone obviously still cares," Erika pointed out.

"But at what cost? At the cost of *whom*? That's the real question. Someone is giving them money to be here, but until I know who that is, I don't trust them."

"You could've asked them that. You could've listened to them and then decided what you wanted to do. If you wanted to have anything to do with them or not." Doris didn't want to mention the mountain god and magic, not wanting to go anywhere near what happened to her yesterday night. Not wanting to give him a confirmation that he was somewhat right in believing the powers above still held some interest in her. It was easier to steer the conversation towards the mundane. There were people here, working on something, and it would be his fault if he missed out on their help out of misplaced pride, not hers.

"I've witnessed so many deaths of medical varieties, viruses, cancers, failed organs. I've buried my parents and grandparents, my younger brother. Saw my nephews die one by one, and only one of them because of someone's carelessness. In all that time, I've witnessed only one medical miracle and it had nothing to do with science." And there he was, getting to that topic even when she'd tried to avoid it. She sighed and accidentally leaned too close to one book stack, making it tumble over. An old paperback, fraying and degrading but protected in the clear plastic cover, fell in a ruffle of pages and crinkling plastic.

"I don't know why it had chosen me," she finally said. So many desperate people want so many things, struggling in life to get them, a lot of time not able to. And there she had been, a trans teen on puberty blockers, saving up money for future surgery, having it all planned out. "I don't know what I did, or didn't do, to get to that place, for my wish to come true." For so many people, the ninth well had only been a folk tale. She knew, intellectually, that there were other people experiencing weird stuff at the time, but for the most part, it wasn't very beneficial to them. People had been getting scared because they dove out among drowned corpses floating on the surface of the sea. They didn't get anything out of it, other than nightmares. Not to mention those who disappeared on the mountain.

And her father hadn't heard of anyone getting to the well and its riches. Who knows, maybe there were more people like her that she simply didn't know about because they all kept it a secret.

"I know. I think, maybe, your belief was purer than most."

She wanted to scoff, wave it away. She wasn't a believer. But she remembered herself as a child, following her father around the small remote villages, absorbing communal tales as surely as a sponge did water. However, it was a normal thing for someone so young. Wouldn't there be more kids dreaming of wells and finding their heart's desires, then?

Before Doris could say anything, her father doubled over, heaving, his hand grasping at his chest.

"Are you alright?" She rushed to his side, put a hand on his shuddering back. It wasn't a coughing fit like yesterday's, it was worse. "I think he can't breathe," she said to Erika who joined her at the other side, having heard the rising panic in Doris' voice. He continued gasping for air, his body trembling under her touch.

"Should we call for an ambulance?" Erika asked.

"You said they weren't in town. The nearest hospital is on the other side of the mountain." The panic was starting to get to her. She felt utterly hopeless, standing there above her grunting father, bent over his knees and shaking through each broken breath he couldn't get to his lungs. There was a wet sound deep in his chest.

The dog noticed something was wrong and he was moving around her father's legs, trying to get a paw on his knees in comfort. Stribor raised his head and sniffed the air near father's head, before letting out a heartbreaking whine.

"Erika, could you move the dog?" she bit out, massaging his back as if it could help somehow. "Dad, please, are there some pills that can help? Could you give us a hint?" He shook his head and the heaving got worse. Her father was suffocating, and she was standing there, a useless witness to his pain.

Erika took the whining dog in her arms, and just in time for Doris' father to start throwing up. If she could call it that. It wasn't bile, nor liquid from his stomach, something he'd been digesting unsuccessfully. What was coming out of his mouth was a thick mass, the dark color of an overripe cherry, and solid. It got stuck in his throat and he couldn't get it out, choking on the fetid matter. He grasped at it and pulled with his fingers, getting more of it out of his body, uncurling it from within like a rope until it plopped on the floor.

The dog whimpered, pathetically, and her father finally stopped shaking, hungrily inhaling deep breaths.

Under him, a clot of sizzling tissue lay on the ground, smelling of cooked entrails.

CHAPTER 4

THE STENCH OF PUTREFACTION was as palpable as the morning fog and it invaded Doris' nostrils as soon as she opened the door to her father's bedroom, with him loosely holding onto her shoulder. He was swaying drunkenly but managed to climb the stairs with her help. She was half fuming, half terrified, the image of bloody insides staining the floor of the living room in front of her face. He was shaken but lucid, and that was the worst part. Because, like this, he refused to go to the hospital, even though his chest still hurt, regardless of what he'd puked out.

Doris helped him cross the room and get to the bed in the obfuscating gloom. It seemed he kept the shutters firmly down everywhere in the house. There was no room for sunlight between the slits. He had no virtual assistants for her to give verbal commands to for the light, so she had to find the old-school giraffe in the dark on his nightstand.

The white artificial light managed to break through the darkness, illuminating her father's head on the pillow. Suddenly, all seventy-seven of his years could be seen on his face and then some; the years had plowed through his skin, leaving deep creases. He was so wizened she thought he could easily crumble into dust, just like his yellowed-paper books stacked in his living room.

When did her father get so old?

In all the time she hadn't talked to him—while she wasn't paying attention—time snuck in and did its thing. Time was the real enemy of everyone and everything. It didn't wait for daughters and fathers to relearn how to communicate, to find common ground. It didn't wait for them to fix their mistakes.

"Are you sure?" she asked, again and again, she stopped counting. "We could drive you, or we could call for the ambulance..." Driving was faster and preferred; they would have to wait a long while for the ambulance to come, which is why there used to be a car with two medics always in the town. *Without people, there was no reason to keep it here*, a voice whispered inside her, sounding like her father. *That's not true, there are still people here*, she said back to the voice.

Just not the ones that count.

"Like it would be any help. I'm screwed either way, so at least let me be at home." The big gray growth on his right cheek undulated with the facial muscles shaping his words. The patch had spread to his right eye's lower eyelid, but she wasn't sure if it had been that large yesterday.

He moved his head and the right eye caught the light of the lamp, reflecting it back, shining white.

"I just need to rest," he said, with a phlegm-heavy sigh. She didn't dare to speak, frozen in the headlights of the impossible reflection in the human eye.

"I know," her father continued as if replying to something she had said. "Thank you... for being here..."

With a shaky movement, she clutched at his frail hand with her bandaged palm. For a moment or two, they held each other like that in silence, and then she left him in his lair, blanketed in darkness. At his closed doors, she stopped and leaned on the wood with her forehead. Tears pricked at her eyes but she refused to let them fall; she would not cry.

With a few deep breaths, Doris could feel herself calming a bit and she straightened up. On the ground floor, she could hear Erika's steps and her low voice; speaking to someone, probably on the phone. Two more doors stood closed on the second storey—one for the bathroom, and one of her old room. That one called to her, a siren luring the tired sailor to stray from their trip home into the warm embrace of the infinity of the sea.

Her legs moved of their own volition, faster than her thoughts. The door opened and, for a moment, her brain conjured the image of a clean but cluttered room, with a huge gaming computer; movie posters on the wall, the desk covered in various headphones for different uses, recorders, a ring light, a state-of-the-art tablet, an e-reader, and even some notebooks. She'd fancied herself a YouTuber, then a podcaster, then streamer—but she was no more than a kid, and the only thing left to her was cringe.

It wasn't what her eyes saw now, and she needed a second for her brain to catch up. The room had been turned into a study, with a big oak desk replacing her old bed. The posters were down and there was a big corkboard with pieces of paper and photos there instead. The only piece of technology visible was a laptop on the desk, but when she ruffled through the drawers, she found hard disks, labeled with dates and locations. The bottom drawer held tapes from an old recorder, long before her time. A lot of file folders, too, as well as notebooks. A white bookcase with glass doors kept ancient, leather-bound books lovingly placed on the shelves. Protected. Her father collected physical books, but she didn't need a bookshelf, only clouds.

On the corkboard, she noticed the printed-out paper sheets telling the story of the ninth well. And not only that, but other versions of the secret, lost treasures on the Velebit range—from the Turks, the Romans, or even the Uskoks who'd stolen it from the Venetians. She traced the stories with her finger, remembering walking with her father to the neighboring villages, listening to the storytellers perform. Entranced with the tales of lost treasures, dead Turks, and werewolves; with the village elders telling them. No one could do it the way the old folk narrators did, the completely mundane people who sat in front of their doors when the summer heat was too high, drinking cool white wine. When she was small, these people were already ancient; their tales on the verge of being forgotten. They used to be passed from generation to generation; now, they were collected in books and records, taught by professors, and analyzed by academics.

Was there still someone in Karlobag who dreamt of the ninth well, or will it all disappear once her father dies and goes into the ground? She had moved away, but the god of the mountain remained. She had to believe that it would be the case with the stories, too.

The folk tales of lost treasures were simple, her father had explained to her while she sat by his legs and drank up his words as if they were as sweet as hot chocolate. People here, on the foot of Velebit, were always dirt poor. They didn't have tourism in their time. They lived off sheep and off the land, and the land wasn't that giving. So, they dreamt of some lost treasure, somewhere hidden, but close to their home, so there was always a chance for them to find it. For their luck to turn.

It was a desperate dream, one only those who had nothing could dream about. And every storyteller that said, *it's the honest truth, our elders knew it*, was sweetening the lie.

The time when she accompanied her father on his research trips was simple and devoid of crippling doubts. She always wondered if she'd gone on to work on synthetic voices because she wanted to recollect that time of childhood joy or to give back to the world the best performance she could help build with her team, just so some other child, used to living with the artificial world at their fingertips, could get a glimpse of greatness she'd once experienced.

Her father thought she was stealing voices from the living, and her company was constantly dragged through the mud in the press about one thing or another—and her childhood had ended up under lock and key in her mind. She kept it all away to function as a relatively normal adult, living a simple mundane life.

In a corner of the corkboard, there was a photo and it jerked her to see it and touch it as an object, not pixels on the screen. The blue in the photo was so clear and light it burned her eyes, and in the vastness of it, two specks of pink, one of them on a bright white unicorn floaty, the other swimming close by. Smiling faces of her father and her—her before she could even form memories, before she chose her name—grasping the neck of the unicorn, while her father's head floated just above the surface, by her side, his hand waving at the camera. Probably to her mother, standing on the dock. They looked so happy in the sea, which was so calm and turquoise and clean.

This is how it used to be between the three of them. An easy acceptance and cozy happiness.

Watching this moment, she now felt too ungrateful, too self-obsessed. *You are more similar to your father than you would admit*, her mother told her countless times, yet she never listened. They had the same blind spots, it seemed, and the same stubbornness. It was thicker than blood.

She took the photo from the wall but didn't have anywhere to put it. Her wallet was fully digital, and the pockets on her shorts were too small, decorative, useless. In the end, she had to put it back on the corkboard and leave it behind.

"How is he?" Erika asked when Doris got back to the living room, phone in her hands. The dog was blinking tiredly at his spot by her father's chair, swaying as if he were slow dancing to music only he could hear. The floor had been cleaned up, but a pink spot marred the tiles.

"Tired, but otherwise strangely fine. I mean, not *fine*, but..." She stopped, struggling to give words to her jumbled thoughts. There was something nagging her, but she couldn't give it form, not in this house. These walls, these rooms, were too drenched in the past, haunting her every waking moment.

"I know what you mean. That wasn't a normal thing to throw up." Erika's voice was trembling, higher by an octave. She was walking in circles like she did when something was bothering her. "'Ris, it looks like some... part of an organ. I don't know, I'm not a doctor."

"I know," Doris said, feeling every second of last night's incident and the consequential lack of sleep.

"How is he not dead?"

"I don't know."

"You can't throw up your insides and just sleep it off."

"And yet, here we are."

"Do you think it's magic?" Erika finally stopped walking and looked directly at her.

Doris shrugged. "I have no idea. The... thing last night insinuated that whatever the fuck is happening is our fault. But I'm not an expert. I was just kidnapped once... sorry, twice now, by a fucking mountain."

"It's a strange way to describe what happened to you, but okay," Erika said, plopping down on the couch.

"It would explain some things," Doris acknowledged. "Everything about this bacteria is strange, even to my high school level of understanding of microbiology." She stood on the verge of a meltdown, while her wife followed her movements with her knowing eyes. Her wife... Doris had dragged to this horrible town. "You should have stayed home. I know mom said we should be okay here, but who knows, I just... what if..."

"Hey, hey." Erika stood up and took Doris' face in her hands. "Enough of that. I'm your partner, your wife, not a fucking piece of furniture for you to leave behind. Whatever happens, happens to both of us. And I wasn't going to leave you to handle all of this heavy emotional shit on your own."

It was getting harder and harder to keep the tears away, but Doris persisted. Her wife's palms were warm on her cheeks, but it wasn't an unwelcome burn. It was comfort and love. She basked in it, soaking in it, like a cat sunbathing on a ruined fortress roof.

"What should I do?" The question was filled with uncertainty, fear, and discomfort. It was as poignant as the stench of decay wafting from the books, from the furniture and damp walls.

"Honestly? I don't know, honey. Maybe nothing. But I know you can't just sit here and fret." Erika shrugged;

such a simple movement that hid a lot of meaning. "I think you should try to talk to your foreigners, to see what they wanted to talk to your father about. They are our neighbors, it shouldn't be hard."

"And what about him?" She nodded towards the first floor.

"I'll stay, keep an eye on him," Erika offered, then scrunched her nose. "I'll also try to ventilate the room and get some light in."

"You don't need to—"

"I want to help," Erika said, as simple as that. "Besides, if I'm staying here, I don't want to choke on stale air." She made a shooing motion with her hand, clearly set on her plan. Doris checked if her phone was on her, then obeyed her wife, who was ready to stay alone in a place drenched with ghosts and two sick, old souls.

The old Danica's house appeared to be empty. Either that or they were ignoring her knocking. Remembering what her wife had told her about the strangers frequently going out to sea, Doris decided to check out the beach. The sun was flaming in the sky without a single cloud, not the best time to be outside, where its radiation was high. Her watch beeped in three short blips, alerting her of its dangerous levels as if she didn't already know that. But she'd made sure to put the straw hat firmly on her head and covered her exposed skin in a thick layer of sunscreen.

The town was as suffocatingly quiet as the day before as if it were the dead of winter, when loneliness was harsher than the cold winds biting through the clothes. Doris kept her eyes on the windows and doors, waiting to see which places were truly empty, and which hid living people inside. She wasn't one for small talk and would usually try to avoid people she knew, but now she found herself itching to see a familiar face. Nineteen years was a lot, and while some old people of her youth were certainly six feet underground—as was old Danica—there should still remain some distant relatives and noisy busybodies who made sure she knew their opinions about her. The town's judgment was never late, always behind a corner, waiting to be delivered. Not everyone had the money and the opportunity to get out of the town.

Only one place, one small café seemed open, but it used to belong to a family that Doris despised, so she made sure to give it a wide berth even though she was curious to see who it was that was working. Was Leon—her childhood bully—still living here and working in his father's place, waiting for customers to brew them bitter coffee? Or was he one of those, like her, who'd managed to run away and was replaced by someone more desperate?

The first actual person she saw, not counting her father or the researchers, was a cashier leaning against the door of a small shop, smoking. She was older than Doris by some twenty years or so, and when her bloodshot eyes found Doris', there was nothing in them. Not a spark of recognition, not a questioning look, not anger, or even annoyance. Her cheeks and long neck were riddled with blue-gray flakes, glistening in the sun. The thin, strawlike hair was striped with grays, hanging limply from her head, patches of it missing. She dragged smoke from the electric device deep into her lungs and then blew it out on autopilot.

Doris couldn't recognize the cashier, not at first glance. But there was a flickering familiarity in the woman's face, one she knew she could place if she concentrated. Before she could do that, sift her memories as if flour, the woman turned back and headed inside the shop.

Shaking off the discomfort, Doris crossed the empty road towards an equally empty parking lot, smaller than the one she'd parked on. This was where she'd sauntered the night before, except now the sun was exposing the sad state of things—the half-church, the empty graveyard behind it, overgrown with lichen and moss, the broken asphalt she'd walked on, the surface of the sea covered in a thick, pinkish muck, rather than shiny bioluminescence. The night washed in the red glow was disturbing but, ironically, it hid the depressive reality confronting her right now.

Anticipating the smell, she put on her synthetic filter mask, kept for emergencies in her bag ever since the last pandemic. Better the weird smell of her captured breath, than to inhale the foulness permeating the air above the water. It didn't block it completely, but it dulled it to a tolerable level, which was enough, even though her breathing became shallower and harder under the heat.

She came to a stop at the same concrete block that people used to sunbathe on, where she'd stood last night, transfixed with the sights. On the right, a small pebble beach extended into a sharp, rocky seabed, boulders protruding out of the water, forming a seawall over the beach, turning it into a smallish cove. The beach was covered in a glittering, translucent substance, and when she squinted, she could make out clusters of bigger, domelike organic matter, scattered all over the beach. The same things that were covering the sea, probably washed out with the tide.

Stone stairs led from her spot to the beach, half of them submerged in the sea. She could see they were mostly ruined now, cracked and broken like teeth spilled from a jaw with a heavy hit.

The concrete beach continued on the left—a short promenade over another small pebbled cove. The long, low structure filled with changing rooms had been in shambles even in her youth, the rusted metal frames devoid of doors—leaving for everyone to see the dirty, tetanus-infested insides. It was a reminder that, even before the sickness, the town had already been in decline. The never-fixed church, the old, bare changing rooms without doors or purpose, the winter stasis; they were all signs of a dying, trapped animal.

The changing rooms were now riddled with cracks like scars, the roof half caved in. She'd missed it last night, focusing on the red light and the sea, but now it was all out in the open for her to see.

Out there, on the water, a lonely boat was rocking lazily. A cabin cruiser, ancient by the looks of it, in need of a new coat of paint; enough for maybe three or four people, depending on how big the inside space was. She couldn't see anyone in it, with the closed cabin facing her.

Knowing that regular people had nothing to do in this filth, Doris decided to wait for a bit and see what would happen. There was no shade in sight for her to hide in, but she had an almost empty tote bag with her, so she took out the bottle of sunscreen and her phone and used it as a cushion on the edge of the beach. The concrete had soaked up all of the scorching heat it could get from the sun and she could feel it radiating through her shorts and the bag. Her legs dangled over the calm water as if she were daring it to do something.

The sun roasted her mercilessly, no matter how much sunscreen she kept spreading on her exposed arms and legs, her watch beeping incessantly. Under her fingers, she could feel her skin tightening and she knew she wouldn't be able to stay under the direct sunlight for long, not if she wanted to have at least one calm night.

A head emerged from the surface, near the boat, covered in translucent mucus. A hand soon followed, grasping at the side of the boat. Doris had the front seat to a diver getting out from the sea, their sleek, dark gray scuba suit full of slime. Since the boat's bow was still facing her, she lost sight of the diver the moment they managed to drag themselves up, but not before she could glimpse something in their other hand; something baggy, wiggling slightly. Unless it had been her vision playing games and it was only a bag filled with trash. Whatever it was, they'd fished something out from underneath the surface, and it sparked her curiosity. The need to know what was happening was strong and she stayed rooted on the spot, even while the sun rays slowly ate through her skin, boiling out the water from her body and leaving pink traces that could very easily turn an ugly red.

The sudden movement in the water at her right drew her attention away from the boat. There was something under the surface, between the grass-covered rocks, a dark shape obfuscated by the layer of muck. She turned towards it slightly, trying to follow its movement, but it was quick and she lost sight of it when it went towards the rock wall, away from her. Was it another diver? Or was it a big fish, or a shark? But what would sharks be doing here in this poison, so close to the shore?

The sea rippled in bubbles at the bottom of the rock wall—the air breaking out from beneath. Bubbles inflated and burst; popping one by one. Something, or someone, was letting out air underwater, disturbing the surface level of filthy muck, almost in rhythm with the blips of her watch.

The loud rumble of an engine was as surprising and as alarming as a sudden thunderstorm on a clear summer day and Doris flinched, catching her chest and feeling the beating heart. It was only the boat coming to life, managing to successfully freak her out while she was waiting for the shadow to dive out from the filth. The cabin cruiser shifted, turned sideways from her, and she saw the diver sitting at the gunwale, with a petite person with a huge hat covering their head—*was that Chloe?*—standing over them. With the engine working, the shifting boat splattered a rain of pink mucus behind itself, as if leaving a trail of bloody tears.

She wasn't a squeamish person, but the sight disturbed her more than she would like; making her ask whether this was what it had looked like when the engine caught her cousin Dorian under its blade. Was his minced face flying through the air while the speedboat kept on rushing, until someone finally saw what was happening? Did these people see what their boat was trailing behind, did they care?

A movement glimpsed out the corner of her eye—just a glittering flash on the rocks—grabbed her attention from her morbid thoughts, before her brain caught up with the quiet splash. The surface of the water rippled in circles before it calmed again as if there was nothing there.

It was just a fish. Doris tried to reason with herself, and yet she stopped breathing, afraid to make a sound, and her legs were two blocks of iron, weighing her down. It now seemed monumentally foolish to sit like this, her feet so close to the sea, right within reach... of what? Her eyes were glued to the rocks and the sea, waiting for another bubble or ripple, or a hint of a shadow passing by. The slime lightly undulated under the sun. Her watch beeped again and she put it on mute, following an instinct to be quiet, invisible. Anything could be down there. Before it was a simple matter of general, uninteresting fish and the occasional anemone rooted in the stones; a stray jellyfish was the most excitement this place could see. The bacteria changed everything—the fish had mutated and died out, her mother had mentioned, there was nothing living under there, there shouldn't be. Yet, she'd seen the shadow, the bubbles. Something lived.

She breathed in a shallow breath, stagnant from the mask. Slowly, her legs moved, getting back on the firm, boiling concrete, on the safe ground, where nothing could reach out to her from the water. The image of a slick purple tentacle grasping at her feet and dragging her down to drown—while absurd, which she was completely aware of—was so clear in her brain she could already feel the dense salty fluid in her mouth, blocking her airway. With careful movements, as if she were taking care not to disturb a sleeping animal, Doris stood up and picked up her things. She wasn't sure what to think, but panic firmly gripped her body in a tight embrace. Dread coiled in the pit of her stomach and she was acutely aware of the oppressive swelter, of her lungs not getting enough air, of the stinging pinpricks breaking out on her skin.

And the surface of the sea bubbled, bulging with a blood-dark shadow ready to break through the muck.

CHAPTER 5

"HI! HEY!" A VOICE called out a greeting to her, high and loud, through the growling of the sputtering engine. The shadow retreated under the surface, quickly disappearing from sight again. Doris breathed in, drenched in sweat and panic. The surface calmed, seemingly undisturbed, peaceful, but she knew better now, could not be deceived by the mucus hiding the secrets of the depths.

A petite figure waved at her from the boat, and they were now close enough for her to see it was, indeed, Chloe. With a dry mouth and stinging eyes, Doris pointed at the sea, unsure of what exactly she wanted to convey. There was something there, she wanted to say, to shout. Or, better yet, she wanted to ask Chloe: *what* was there? She'd seen Chloe's colleague diving, and seen them getting something out from the sea.

They had to know what was hiding there, what lived in the toxic waste; whatever could survive there. Why was she so afraid, suddenly? Of something that could only be some huge deformed fish? It surely wasn't reason enough for her to feel like this, for her heart to beat so fast, her arms and legs get covered in thousand painful pinpricks. It was just her nerves getting to her, clearly blowing things out of proportion, convincing her mind there was a danger lurking in the sea, where in fact, the true threat was microscopic and impossible to see with one's naked eyes.

The boat went for the small dock on the other side of the beach that Doris currently stood on. She followed it, thirsty for answers, while also, probably, literally dehydrated.

Doris came to the edge of the pier, peeking inside the boat in hope of catching some sort of clue, jittering with nervous energy. Several people stood inside, including Chloe and Tendai, whom she'd already met. The guy she'd seen smoking in the window was standing at the helm, and there was the fourth person, a diver who sat on the deck with their suit still on, covering every inch of them, the breathing mask resembling an astronaut helmet more than the usual diver equipment. At their waist, a belt held various devices, including a short, prong-ended baton and a hook. Under their legs was a writhing, sleek bag, still wet.

She remembered seeing an aquarium at the shack on the mountain and again wondered, for a moment, what were they doing there.

"Hi there! Nice to see you again." Chloe's hello seemed genuine, even under the filter mask she also wore. Her eyes were twinkling with a smile. Even Tendai waved at Doris, much more relaxed than he was the night before. The man from the window went to tie the boat to the dock, but it was obvious his attention was firmly on Doris.

All three of them wore full-body coverings, similar to diving suits, rubbery and dark blue. A subtle logo was printed on the right side of their chests and she recognized it as a well-known multinational company with fingers in all of the pies—from technology, energy, and entertainment, to the military industry and space exploration.

Her suspicion instantly flared—they weren't known for their philanthropic nature. Anyone that gets that big rarely is.

"What's in the sea? I saw something moving," Doris ignored Chloe's greeting and didn't bother with pleasantries. Instead, she let her voice hold a tinge of a frantic intensity mixed with firmness. She's not going to be ignored.

"You saw something?" the smoking man asked in a raspy voice behind the mask. "Can you be a bit more specific?"

"Something was in the water, underwater. Big. Swimming. It went for the rocks." All four of them turned towards her. She was sure that even the eyes of the diver—only the faintest outline of them visible—hidden behind the murky, shaded ball of a breathing mask, were set on her.

"It's probably a jellyfish," the man finally said, with the tone of a parent, or a mentor, used to being in charge. His accent was a bit harder to place.

"Jellies are mostly translucent, there's no way I would've been able to see it. Not that big." The dome-like head of a jellyfish, breaking the surface of the water, didn't really fit with what she thought she'd seen trying to get to the surface, but she wasn't sure anymore. Weren't there medusas that floated on the surface? Besides, it didn't get far enough for her to get a clear look at it. Maybe it really was just a jelly emerging from the depths. "What did *you* see?" She'd reserved the last part for the diver.

They ignored her question, sitting there like a statue, with a dark wet silicon bag under their legs. The content squirmed, almost imperceptibly, but Doris was sure she saw it move. It was big enough to hold a school of saddle bream, like it were a fishing boat that had come back with a bountiful catch, and she was here to buy the fresh meat. Whatever it was in there, Doris doubted it was the fish.

"Let's go, Kai needs to decontaminate," the man said, giving out orders. Anger flared in her, heated up by the incessant sun, scorching her from the outside in.

"*Pička ti materina*," she cursed him in Croatian, and by Tendai's surprised, strangled laugh she could safely guess he understood her. Curses were the first Croatian words strangers usually learned. He turned his laughter into a cough, or tried to, under the heated look the man gave him.

"You know, I'll stay with you for a bit. Explain what you want to know," Chloe said, taking off the upper part of her suit. With her neck exposed, Doris could see the tattoo, in bright neon colors. Even in the day, she wasn't sure what it was supposed to be. "Come, let me show you something," Chloe continued, picking up a purple rucksack and a tiny silver telescopic stick, and disembarking.

"Chloe—" the man started, but Chloe interrupted him.

"It'll be fine, she has a right to know, and it's not a big secret. Come," she repeated at Doris, motioning for her to follow. The man wasn't impressed and clearly wanted to say something, but ended up cut off by Tendai catching his arm and whispering to him. Doris wasn't certain, but she thought she could hear *need to go fast before...* But Chloe caught her hand and started dragging her away from the boat, her mysterious colleagues, and the bag's questionable contents.

Trash didn't have a tendency to move. Maybe it was really just diseased fish and they used fancy bags instead of nets.

The two of them got back to the same concrete beach where Doris had been looking at them from, so she couldn't see the rest of them disembark. It was obviously deliberate, and a very successful distraction. If it were left to the man in charge and his rude dismissal, Doris would still be standing there, yelling at them. Chloe had managed to get her away quietly, and she hadn't even blinked.

Still, Chloe wanted to speak to her, and that was something.

"Sorry for Dr. Kinkade. He's not the most... welcoming person," Chloe said, extending out a stick ending in prongs.

"I know people like him," Doris said.

"Yeah, I met your father. I mean, if I guessed correctly, your dad is Dr. Vrban? You mentioned him dying, and well, you have his... er... demeanor."

"You can drop the title, we don't really use it for people with a PhD here in Croatia, it's reserved for MDs."

"Well, Dr. Kinkade isn't an MD, and he would flay us if we called him *mister*. But, I think this riveting honorifics discourse isn't what you wanted to talk about. Look at this."

Chloe crouched over the edge of the concrete, reaching over with the stick. The prong went through the reddish muck covering the surface. She stirred a bit, as if she were cooking, before getting the stick out at an angle. Hanging from its elongated metal form was a shapeless, translucent blob.

"Do you know what this is?" Chloe asked while the blob was sliding from the stick.

"I thought it was just some secretion. Trash covering the sea and the beach."

"If it had tentacles, you would probably recognize it more easily. This is what we call a gelatinous organism."

"It's a medusa?"

"Well, no. Medusa is a jellyfish, but they aren't the only form of gelatinous organisms. These babies don't have any stinging cells. They are, well, a type of the gelatinous plankton, like the *Mnemiopsis leidyi*—comb jelly—you know, those you have in the Istria region?"

"Those invasive jellies that killed the majority of our fish?" Doris didn't know a lot about them, not that interested in that part of Croatia, not even when she lived here. But she had a friend in college who was from Istria, and they sometimes mentioned how messed up a feeling it was to swim among the jellies, but how it was even worse on their fisherman.

"I wouldn't use the word *kill*... they are predators, but so are wolves, and I'm not sure you would say they kill the sheep."

"The jellies obliterated our native species," Doris said, remembering what she'd heard about it.

"It is actually quite beautiful to dive among them with a mask. They have this bioluminescence and aren't interested in humans. They only eat other zooplankton, fish eggs, and larvae, and they lack stinging cells, so you can touch them without fear."

"Okay, fine, so, they are shiny, glittering invasive predators, not dangerous for humans, only a blight for the fishermen. But this thing right there?" Doris showed with her hand. "It looks sickly. Not cute. Not even like an organism, for that matter. It looks like a plastic bag that went through a whale's digestive system." As if to show Chloe how right Doris was, the jelly on the stick plopped from it into the sea. And Chloe was here telling her that this surface-level layer of muck was actually a cluster of living beings.

Doris turned towards the beach where dozens of these creatures were rotting on the pebbles, coughed out from the sea onto dry land, left to the sun. No wonder the town smelled of rotten fish.

"You're right about that. They're sick," Chloe said and stood up, straightening her back. "It's not normal for them to float on the surface. And to cluster in this particular way. Also, their bioluminescence isn't red, and it's not that strong. That light you can see in the night? That's all the bacteria."

"Bacteria have bioluminescence?" Doris only knew what she'd learned in her high school biology lessons, and she had to wreck her brain to remember even that much.

"Yep. Bioluminescent bacteria is what you can find in the sea, on the surface of fish carcasses or in the gut of other marine animals. Though it's not usually this... strong."

"You don't say. And here I remember using decaying fish instead of lamps." Sarcasm sweetened Doris' voice, but Chloe only shrugged, apologetically.

She retracted the telescopic stick, parts of it covered in slime. "Marine bacteria isn't my area of expertise, that's Tendai's specialty, so my professional opinion on the matter would be that this bioluminescence is really freaky. What I can tell you is about these poor jellies." Chloe pointed at the surface. "Okay, so, jellies love warmer water, and climate change means they're showing up where they've never been present before. It's not uncommon for them to come with ballast water, too—which is how you get them in new places. They hitch a ride on a ship, and when you have a crowded sea space, well—"

"Like in Istria." Which was a much more popular tourist destination than Karlobag.

"Exactly, like there. What's interesting, though, is the fact that we can't be sure how these jellies came here, or what attracts them to this place. But we know one thing. They are all infected."

"With the same thing that's killing my dad." The world titled in a vertigo-inducing spell. Too late, Doris remembered that she hadn't eaten anything all morning. Her stomach grumbled and the time she'd spent with a mask on didn't help—she was lightheaded and nauseous, and she was sick of feeling like that. It had started the moment she came back, like a twisted thorny twine of anxiety constricting over her intestines with every breath she took. And it wasn't stopping, only getting worse and worse; her body was on the verge of puking her soul out with each new information. She understood words that were coming out of Chloe's mouth, but they sounded more nebulous than her time with the ancient mountain powers.

"Exactly." Chloe nodded. Big drops of sweat were gliding over her forehead and she took her hat off to wipe it away. From that angle and without a hat hiding it, Doris could see the slight scar in the buzz of the undercut behind Chloe's ear. It was a clean, vertical incision, and even though she had no proof it was the case, it screamed 'neurolink placement'. The only ones in existence and safe for people to have inserted were from the same corp whose logo Doris saw on the suits, which they loved to boast about, promising a future where their consumers could easily be connected to the whole wide world.

Doris had thought it was not commercially available, yet. They had barely stopped killing the monkeys a few years back.

Chloe put the hat back and the pink, irritated-looking scar disappeared under it.

"You said bacteria was Tendai's specialty. What's yours?" Doris asked, her mind still on the possible neurolink, trying to find the connection between this corporation, Chloe, and what was happening in her old town. She couldn't think of any positive reason for the giant to have an interest in them.

"I'm a doctoral candidate in marine biology, with an interest in gelatinous zooplankton, specifically."

"You're here for the jellies." Doris was dumbfounded. It made sense with the way Chloe talked about jellies, but, for some reason, it didn't cross Doris' mind that would be Chloe's area of expertise. Doris hadn't even known about there being gelatinous organisms of interest, only flesh-eating bacteria currently wrecking her father's insides. And there was no funding for epidemiologists or a cure—but there was for marine biologists to research the sick jellies.

Her father had mentioned they weren't here for him. She hated that he was being proven right.

"In a manner of speaking," Chloe said.

"Why did you even want to talk to my dad?"

"Oh, he mentioned us? I guess, not in a good light." Chloe visibly cringed. "Look, it's just a bunch of questions we asked the others, too, but he was of the biggest interest to us as an index case. He was the first to be recorded showing signs of the infection, even though we can't be sure if, in actuality, he had been the first to catch the bacteria. The earliest documentation is about him, though, so we work with that."

The infested jellies rested calmly on the water. It was easier to watch them than Chloe's mask-covered face. Besides, her voice was far easier for Doris to decipher than the existence of the things on the water. Currently, she sounded exasperated. With whom? Doris' father?

"We thought he could help us clear up the timeline. It's currently a mess. We don't know for sure when the bacteria first showed up, we don't know for sure when the first jelly came. It's a new species of both, you know, newly discovered. Yet, the jellies didn't spawn here, in this very visible cluster. Days, maybe weeks passed before swimmers noticed a few here and there. It wasn't until your father came to the doctor with a small skin deformity that anyone had any idea something was different. And it was months and countless referrals before someone got an idea of what was happening, and only because more cases kept popping out in the meantime. By the time the jellies became so numerous they were forming a thick surface coat, we had the name for the bacteria."

By that time, it was too late for a lot of people. With high summer heat, everyone along the coast had gone swimming to cool off. Town elders, adults, children. Not just of this town, but the visiting tourists, too. Hundreds of people, a lot of them not even local, walked around with gray scales growing over their bodies, their organs slowly melting away. Too bad no one was an important celebrity, influencer, or oligarch. Mostly, they were just regular people, with regular lives.

"So we asked, well, tried to ask your father if he remembered anything particularly interesting happening six years ago, *before* he noticed the unnatural skin growth. Anything different, out of the ordinary, strange."

"Hm." The earthquake was the first thing that popped into Doris' mind. The biggest one that has ever shaken Croatia, turning a whole city into dust and crippling the already bumbling government.

"But he wasn't very forthcoming. He told Dr. Kinkade to stuff a sea cucumber up his ass... not that he could find one, even if he wanted to."

"What happened to the cucumbers?"

Chloe shrugged. "It appears the jellies ate them."

Doris blinked and waited for a second, then two, believing Chloe will start laughing at the apparent joke. But she didn't. She stayed like that, dead serious.

"Do *you* have any ideas?" Chloe asked, carefully. She was watching Doris intently, sweat dripping on her eyebrows and drenching the edges of the mask. Doris had to take another moment, to stop thinking about a plastic bag devouring a sea cucumber as big as her forearm, before answering.

"Why do you even care about that? Why is that important?" Doris said with her own question. The earthquake had been a very public, very well-recorded event, as were the subsequent humanitarian and economic crises, so she was fairly certain Chloe already knew about that.

Chloe sighed. How much information will Doris be able to get out of her, before Chloe decides it was too much and shuts up? "We... just... want to know how this all started. To better understand what's happening."

Well, Doris couldn't fault her for the vague statement.

It didn't escape Doris' notice that the only reason she knew who employed the researchers was due to glimpsing at their suits. Instead of the logo being splashed all over some big golden yacht for them to cruise on for everyone to see, they were using a nondescript boat. There were only four of them, at least on site—who knows how many worked in some lab somewhere—easy not to disturb what little life was left in the town. No one knew about their involvement. Doris' suspicion about the intentions of the corp was as high as the sun currently roasting her alive.

She didn't expect Chloe to spill everything they were doing like they were best friends. Still, she had to ask. "Why? What do you hope to achieve?" But even as she spoke, it became obvious the question wasn't one Chloe could answer.

She started shaking her head, clearly uncomfortable.

"Can you at least tell me if you have some theories? Why did this happen, I mean."

At this, Chloe visibly relaxed. "Oh, there's few, I'm sure you saw it all on the net." Chloe raised her right index finger. "Climate change is the usual suspect. But if this had anything to do with the absorption of carbon dioxide, we would see more cases like this somewhere else. That's not even counting all the weirdness. Since it's a contained case" —she raised the middle finger— "it could be some sort of pollution or chemical spill."

"Like the case of *E. coli* in the southern Adriatic," Doris murmured, mostly to herself. It happened when she was a child. On the southern coast of Croatia, *Escherichia coli* infested a patch of the sea, thanks to the illegal draining of the septic tanks by the people living in a small coastal town. It was cheaper to dump their shit into the streams—which ultimately found their way to the sea—and for the punishment, they ended up literally swimming in their own feces, with a permanently polluted coast.

Was this something similar? It was a normal thing for tourists to dump their trash into the sea, but it was also quite regular for the locals to do something equally foolish for their leisure or a bigger profit. Karlobag had a functioning sewage system, at least.

"Yeah, like that," Chloe confirmed. "Which is what most people believe happened. We should still know what caused it, be it a leak in sewerage, or someone, I don't know, using the sea as a dumping ground for old computers. But we don't. Which is where we come to more... murkier waters." Chloe giggled at her own pun, but it was subdued. She dropped her hand by her side and stopped counting. "There was a huge seismic event a few months before your father's medical record." So she knew, as Doris suspected.

"It wasn't close, but they still felt it here," Doris confirmed, her eyes drawn to the abandoned changing rooms with their caved-in roof. All of Croatia had felt it.

"Yeah... and, well, we can't be sure that there's a connection. But..." Chloe's eyes became unfocused. She wasn't looking at Doris anymore; whatever she saw, it was inside her mind. "Rowan believed there was a connection. The seabed cracked and something got loose." The last sentence was so quiet, uncertain, that Doris had to strain to hear her talk. She almost barked a laugh but managed to stay still, hoping Chloe would continue her tale before deciding it was enough. She didn't even want to ask who the fuck Rowan was. "But that's a bit insane, isn't it?" Chloe laughed—shortly and hesitantly—like she tried to brush it off, but whoever Rowan was and whatever they believed obviously rankled Chloe. She wasn't indifferent towards this theory.

"Insane? What would be insane? What do you think got out of this crack? Bacteria? How would it even work?"

Chloe was shaking her head. "No, forget it. It's probably nothing. It probably has something to do with the sea's growing acidity. Climate change does *change* a lot of things." Again, nervous laughter.

"But you believe there's something more here. Chloe, what did I see there? It wasn't a fucking jellyfish. It was big and it moved." And all this talk, of jellies and pollution and earthquakes, what was it, a distraction? From what, exactly? To get Doris away from the boat and its content, of the fact that her father was dying and no one gave a damn? Did Chloe believe Doris could possibly be a threat or was she just a kind person sharing what she was able to, with someone that she saw was in need of help? Was she divulging what she could out of pity? Probably.

"I honestly don't know," Chloe said, and by the desperation in it, Doris knew she wasn't lying. She remembered Erika mentioning there being a fifth member of the group, the one that disappeared, and the bloody boat that was left behind. Was that this Rowan person Chloe mentioned? What happened to them? "But if you want my honest opinion, and this won't sound very scientific—I would say that whatever is happening here isn't *normal*. Isn't natural. I know I sound... delirious."

Doris wanted to say it was nothing that would surprise her personally. Wanted to say, *Hey, remember seeing me last night up there on the mountain? I was transported there by powers I can't comprehend and years ago they made some changes to the body I was born with. I'm prepared to believe in anything.* It was a shame she didn't know any sea-related folklore. People from Velebit's foothills were oriented toward the mountain and agriculture.

But the mountain could not help them now. It never could, not really. It could only absorb the dreams and hopes of the people spilling sweat and blood on its ground.

Doris didn't say any of that. She wasn't in the mood to comfort the other woman. Didn't think she deserved that. For the first time, she understood how her father felt when he watched her. She couldn't be sure what sort of business these researchers were doing, but she was more and more doubtful about it being helpful to the people of the town. Everything was too shady for her taste. Chloe might've been a good person, but she was still complicit in whatever morally dubious plan her employer had, and for what, an opportunity to research a bunch of sick jellies?

Or maybe Doris was too jaded, in her father's image. Too cynical after her own experience with the churning of big companies.

"You forgot one," Doris said.

Chloe's brows furrowed. "Forgot what?"

"Theory. The most popular of all." The one that always popped up, no matter the event. "That it's man-made." It's what the mountain had said, isn't it? Or, well, insinuated. "Like people believed about Covid. You know, someone played in the laboratory, made a bacteria, spilled it into the sea." Why would they ever come to Karlobag was another question. None of the theories made a lot of sense. Well, not on their own. Maybe the truth was a mix of them all. A bit of climate change to transform the acidity and warmth of the sea, to make it the perfect living ground for bacteria that slipped out from some hidden place in the seabed, possibly influenced by something fantastical, like a sea god—if there was a mountain power, maybe the sea had its own—enraged by the suffocating amounts of plastic, oil, and trash contaminating the waters. It was a bit of a childish thought, but why not?

In the end, the only thing missing was for a big corp

with secret motives to try and find a way to exploit it for profit, only to accidentally cause it to spread out even more.

She could imagine it all. And… it was pointless. Her father was still infected. The town was still effectively lost. The only things that would remain were the ruins and the cats.

"You don't believe that. What would be the motivation for anyone to do something like that?" Chloe's voice brought her back to the present.

Doris suddenly felt bone tired and emotionally exhausted. Her father would say, without a doubt, *What was the cause for anything in this world?* Money. Power. "You know what, it doesn't matter how it started. Not to me. To me personally, it only matters how it ends."

And there was a sick, wrecked man lying in bed, waiting for a magical cure, and her wife taking care of him because she was loving and kind like that, and maybe Doris didn't deserve her, not that she wanted to think about that. This conversation was interesting, the bits that Chloe was willing to share, and even the hint of a mysterious Rowan and past tense used to talk about them made her curious to learn more—to hear it all, like stories of old.

But ultimately, it was useless to her. She wasn't some superhero to try and save the town. What could she do? Talk to the news crews about what she saw here? Make a fuss on social media? Break into the shack, steal some equipment, take photos of whatever was in the aquarium? She's never even been an activist. She always preferred her own comfort and safety over fighting for ideals or community. To be a cog in the machine, a ghost. If people can't perceive her, she can live in peace.

Now, she felt it was too late to do something meaningful.

Only accept whatever was coming for them. The guilt and anxiety churned in her.

"For what is worth... I'm sorry. About your father. About the town. I truly am. I hope... I hope we will find... something that will help," Chloe said, sounding sincere.

"Thank you, but that's as meaningless as having a disease-infested sea in the summer." Chloe jerked, stricken, but Doris couldn't find it in her to care for her own harsh tone. "Thank you for this illuminating chat, but I need to go back home."

She always believed that the night she dreamt of the ninth well was the most hopeless she's ever been. But if she were honest with herself, that feeling had never dissipated. She'd tried to run away, to leave it behind her, but the hopelessness stayed, rooted in her gut. With her every waking moment, she was constantly reminded of her own limits, but she refused to engage with this emotion, knowing she could slip into despair.

This was just another domino in a line of other dominoes waiting to fall down on her in a chain reaction and crush her beneath their humongous weight. A rushing tide that swept her in to drown her.

The town was waiting silently for her to decide what to do next, while the jellies bobbed lazily on the surface of the sea, sizzling in the sun like vomit.

CHAPTER 6

DORIS NOTED THE NOTIFICATION on her muted watch, walking through the equally quiet town. Where houses stood a soundless watch, like granite gravestones marking the last resting place. Her legs moved unbearably slowly—she was in no hurry to come back and see the state of her father's decline. The display of her watch showed a flashing urgent message, not from Erika, no, she would've called if something had happened, but from work. That stopped Doris on her crawl back, on a narrow street with a dead tree rising from the broken asphalt.

Her work... it was so removed, so far away, hidden by a cloud of clustered blobs. Her life outside this town, her current home in Ireland, daily routines, the time she spent listening to the clips of words spoken by no one real—it all felt like a dream she was just now waking up from. All of her motions were turned insignificant in the face of time rushing past her to the finish line. Only Erika's presence was a certain light, the only shape in Doris' mind that made any sort of sense. No matter how fake everything else seemed now, Erika was, at least, real. And waiting for her to come back.

Doris erased the message. It couldn't be more important than the last branch of her family slowly breaking away from the tree, decaying. It couldn't be more important than the people she loved.

Passing by an open café, the same one she'd tried to avoid before, with a few shaky chairs and tables arranged outside—playing the role of a functional terrace, like everything was still right and there would be locals to sit down for a cup of ice coffee or cold, bitter beer—Doris noticed an ancient man sitting on a tall barstool. His body fat and muscles had been melted down to the bones, the wrinkled old skin of his bald head, neck, and arms covered in bloated gray scales. He was leaning over the table, nursing a beer bottle, and only by the way his gummy jaws munched at the top of the bottle did she recognize him. Barba Vinko.

Barba Vinko had been a town elder even when she was a child. Always sitting at this café, drinking beer, uncaring of the world around him, waiting for his day to fall asleep and never wake up. Somewhere in the back of her mind, she had already written him off, believing he must've died in the last nineteen years, just like old Danica. Instead, here he was, still sitting at the barstool, not dead, but nearly so. And at what cost?

"Doris?" A voice broke through her focus, moving her attention away from the old man ravaged by the strange new bacteria. She got the answer to her previous musings over who was running this place. The man approaching her from the café wasn't someone she wanted to see; of course it would be her childhood bully.

"Leon," she said with a tired acceptance.

"I thought I saw you passing by, but I couldn't be sure." He stopped in front of her, awkward. He was a few years older than her, but in a town with not a lot of children to begin with, that didn't mean much.

The years had passed, and in front of her was not a bored, sneering teenager, with puckered skin overgrown with acne, but a man who looked older than his years, with a gaunt face covered in gray specks. His arms displayed huge growths, like spilled oil, growing over and devouring the ink of his tattoos.

What should she say to him? *It's good to see you again* would be a lie. Especially given the state he was in. But while she wrecked her brain for a reply that would be indicative of the years that had passed like an expanding pit between them, he seemed to recover first.

"I honestly believed I was crazy, you know, why would you come here? Now when everything's going to shit."

"I came to see dad," she said, an easy reply.

He snorted. "Yeah, I figured. But you shouldn't have." It didn't have the biting tone she would've expected from him, it wasn't a threat. It was a statement, as if he were talking about which beer tasted better. "Everyone who was able to has run away, and you, instead, came running *back*. Insane."

"Not everyone. Not my dad, not you." She heard the truth in his words and it rankled her. *Ran back*. And here she was, a few minutes ago, thinking how she'd finally woken up to the real world.

"Only because I can't." He shrugged, his eyes watery, feverish. "I can't afford it. Our house, our café, it's all worth shit. Who would buy property in a cursed town?" Leon leaned forward as if he were about to share a secret with her. "Besides, it's all moot point, anyway. All of us..." He waved his hand, encompassing his face and body, putting himself in the spotlight. "It doesn't matter where we go, how far. We could go north until the skies lit up with the northern lights. It still wouldn't matter. It's in us, and wherever it goes, we take it with us."

She knew he was talking about the bacteria in his

system, but it also felt like he was talking about something deeper than that.

"You should've made your old man come to you, let him die in peace in some fancy hospital. It's too late for him and me. But you got away just in time. Why risk that?"

"Have you met my dad?" she joked, wanting to lighten up the mood, but it felt flat. "I didn't know how bad it was," she finally admitted. It was one thing to hear her mother's reports, another to see it with her own eyes, experience it with her own senses.

"Well now you saw, so what are you waiting—"

A loud crash cut off his sentence, followed by a surprised yelp. Barba Vinko was on the ground, clutching his head with shaking hands. They both rushed towards him, and Doris crouched in front of the old man.

"Barba Vinko, are you alright? Will you let us look at your head?" she said, carefully modulating her voice to give only the impression of calm, hiding the panic inside her chest.

"Barba Vinko, please," she could hear Leon at her side, grasping at the old man's hands, gently moving them away to see the damage.

Her heart dropped right into the pit of her stomach and she thought she would puke out bile into her mask. Leon's sharp intake of breath showed his surprise as well. Barba Vinko's cataract eyes were blinking fast, his mouth opening and closing in silence.

"Who are you?" He asked her, his eyes unfocused, confused.

"She's Vrban's kid, do you remember her? She came to see her dad," Leon answered, a bit dazed. Both Doris and he stood there, uselessly, while the old man bled on the ground.

"Her?" Barba Vinko asked, still confused, and Doris's gut clenched. "Oh, yeah, yeah, Vrban's girl. Doris." He reached with his palms towards her, to touch her face, and she flinched back.

Leon jumped in and took his hands. "Let's get you up, barba."

Doris looked on as if a part of an audience to some strange play being performed in the town square. Detached from her body, this place and time. Her eyes fixed on the wound on the old man's head. The way it wept milky-white fluid, from the cut that had split open his forehead, instead of blood.

It smelled of spoiled fish.

She came back to the house in a haze, her thoughts firmly set on the white slime which ended up covering the old man's face, playing what had happened on repeat. Barba Vinko had waved Leon away, refusing his help, and started sputtering vile phlegm all over his flailing arms. In front of a distraught Doris and Leon, he'd managed to stand up and hobble away, one leg awkwardly dragging along the ground. Almost boneless, rubbery.

That leg and that white, bloodless fluid haunted her steps all the way to the open red door, where she was about to collide with Erika's frightened face.

"You're here! I was just about to call you!"

"I'm alright," Doris said, tasting bitterness on her tongue. Somewhere along her walk, she'd removed her mask, yet she couldn't inhale deeply enough to fill her lungs. "Wait, what, is dad okay?" Her brain finally caught up to her eyes. To Erika's jittery movements, how she was unable to stand still, her warm eyes shining with tears.

"I lost the dog," Erika said in a rush. "I don't know how, he's so old and slow, he was sleeping all the time, but then I looked around and I couldn't find him anywhere."

"Wait, you can't find the dog? He's probably hiding somewhere, he couldn't have disappeared." Unless he melted away in the cracks, she thought, humorlessly. Leaving behind a trail of thick white muck.

"Doris, why do you think the door was open? I was trying to air out the ground floor. I opened the windows and the door to make a draft."

Focusing on the present seemed to come with a struggle; Doris was slowly breaking through the fog in her mind, like a diver drifting towards the surface. So many things were dragging her down, down, towards the seafloor. Everything Chloe had said, the logo, the boat, the white fluid instead of blood seeping out from the head injury.

"He's an old dog, where could he have gone to?" she wondered aloud, grasping for thoughts. It felt so weird to be in her skin right now, hard stretched over muscle and bone, dry and pink from too long in the scorching sun.

"The dock!" Erika almost yelled and rushed down the street, brushing Doris' limp body aside. She was so tired, her legs unsteady. Her stomach was a void, draining her of energy. A wish to lie down and forget about life for an hour or two burned deep inside her heart. But Erika was already disappearing from sight, and Doris didn't trust this town. With a deep, weary sigh, she prayed that the bloody dog was worth it, and went after her wife.

Erika had been right—Doris could see the dog limping towards the dock with determination. His gray, scaly body, with tufts of unkempt fur that stubbornly sprouted between the unnatural growths, seemed even worse in direct sunlight—every inch of his haggard state obvious when brought to the light. Some of the spots seemed swollen, as if filled with water, threatening to burst out. He was in such a sorry state, half alive, half already dead, yet relentless in his trip towards the dock where he'd always waited for his former master—his rescuer, his friend—to come back.

Doris blinked away tears, hit with a wave of nausea and nostalgia so strong she could see her cousin Dorian there, in the sea, beckoning to his dog with a clear booming voice and a ball in his hand. Out of all cousins, he was her favorite, the only one she could claim to have been friendly with. And she could see him now, with his sandy blond hair and a smile stretching wide. Except, he'd gone on a dive and his grin was split open by the blades of a speedboat.

The bloated face waiting for them simply couldn't be his.

Erika stopped in front of Doris, almost in the middle of the road, suddenly still.

"What the fuck," she echoed Doris' sluggish thoughts. "Do you see this too?"

The dog was walking, haltingly but steadily, not towards the docks, as she'd thought earlier, but towards the figure at the surface of the sea. If she could call it that. There was only a head jutting out of the water, bell-like, bloated, slimy, and gray, jellies stuck on its bald head. Two beady black eyes glittered above one round, lipless hole. The thing didn't have a nose, yet there was a bulge in the skin, reminiscent of one existing once upon a time.

"I'm guessing this isn't one of your dead Turks," Erika whispered to Doris when she caught up to her. Doris shook her head.

"We're not in Lomivrat, and they usually just... float. Dead. This... this..." *This didn't even look human*, but she couldn't bring herself to finish the sentence.

"Stribor!" For a brief moment, Doris thought that Erika's frantic call was meant for the thing in the sea before she finally remembered it was the dog's name. It was a futile gesture; he continued his slow-paced trek towards the bobbing head. The dog was deaf, she remembered her father saying.

But he had to be following some urge, some sense they didn't feel, because this can't have been a coincidence. Deeply growing dread started spreading its branches inside her, gripping her tight in its embrace. The two glassy eyes were set on her, shining with amusement. She wasn't sure how she knew that—the thing didn't have a human face, its round hole for a mouth didn't look like something that could smile—yet she knew the thing was enjoying watching them squirm. Doris could feel its enjoyment under her skin like an annoying itch she couldn't scratch. Again, she felt stripped of humanity, turned into a show for a thing outside of this world. Another domino to crush her with its weight. And that finally broke through the paralyzing fear, through nausea and fatigue, stoking the embers of the angry fire that always resided deep inside of her.

Doris hurried toward the damn dog—already so close to the edge of the dock she could see him falling into the water and into the round mouth waiting for him—and picked him up in her arms. The light faded in the glossy eyes that had never stopped looking at her. Translucent jellies were slowly sliding over its oval head; some hanging towards the sea like a cheap wig, hooked to its skin in a way she couldn't understand. Stribor trashed in her hands, trying to break free, but she held onto him with a sure grip. Where she squeezed, the gray patches on his skin wept with white slime, leaving wet trails over her exposed arms. The scales were rough to the touch, scraping her while she held onto him hard.

Even more liquid drizzled from the cracks between the scales, diffusing the overpowering sour stench. She managed to stay still, rather than fainting—from the strain, the smell, from general nausea that had been following her all day—remaining upright and keeping a hold on the dog only by the strength of her pettiness. The thing was waiting for her to fall, and she would not give it the satisfaction. While it remained in the sea, and she on the solid land, it couldn't do anything to them except give them the dirty eye. If it wants the dog that much, it can swim out from the sea and try to get it. If it can.

The round black hole opened wide, showing rows and rows of sharp teeth, resembling a leech. One limp jelly completed its sliding path and dropped right down into the sea with a quiet *plop*.

Erika's footsteps, the dog's haggard breathing, and her own rushing blood were as loud in her ears as the engine of a dozen yachts. Doris didn't dare to breathe, in fear of inhaling the smell deep into her lungs. Afraid it will finally sucker punch her into losing the grip on the dog, or even consciousness. If she fell, would she tumble straight into the sea, into the waiting gaping hole filled with the small, sharp teeth? Were there more of these things in the sea? Each gelatinous blob rocking on the surface could be attached to a head similar to this, hiding a hungry mouth and noseless face.

How have the researchers missed this? Have they? Or was this something Chloe didn't have permission to talk about? Did she mean this thing, when she said she didn't know what was down there?

They had a diver, surely, they would see it swimming underwater? And they'd dragged something out, something Chloe didn't want Doris to see. In her mind's eye, Doris could see a bloated gray baby, with no legs or arms, but with a round, sharp mouth and two eyes like coals, put into an aquarium. Prepared especially for it, close by, but far enough from the sea. She could see blood on the boat, swaying gently in the middle of the night.

Why her mind conjured exactly these images—she couldn't be sure. But the sun was piercing through her hat, straight to her brain, and the lack of air and food was getting to her, making her jump to conclusions. Imagine things.

The rows of teeth were circling the mouth; one, two, three, an infinity of them, expanding and contrasting in a pulsating rhythm. They were rocks on the mountain, the rocks at the bottom of the sea. Behind them, in a pink membrane of a throat, grew colonies of polyps. Doris wanted nothing more than to touch them, feel the sensation under her fingers, check out if it was like corals. If she could make jewelry out of this tender throat, open so wide it could devour her whole if she fell.

"Can you see? It's beautiful," Erika said, at Doris' side, with reverence and fear. Doris became aware of the sensation of dread and heat, of the incessant itching in her arms. Her wife's voice was dreamy. Could Doris see what exactly?

She turned towards Erika, her wife's brown eyes looking at nothing at all, luscious black locs crowning her head and shoulders. Erika moved slightly closer to the edge of the dock and didn't look like she planned to stop.

"Erika? Honey, stay back," Doris called, panic starting to flow with her blood. Erika didn't seem to hear her, continuing in her trance. Her father's angry welcome flashed in Doris' mind, and if something happened to Erika because of her, she would not be able to continue to live with herself. "Stop that RIGHT NOW!" she yelled with a force grown from terror, catching Erika with one hand, while she still kept hold of the dog with the other.

It did the trick. Erika jolted awake as if she'd been napping on the couch in the safety of their home. She blinked away the nothingness from her eyes and her mouth formed an O, on a smaller scale, but similar to the sea thing's gaping mouth.

"I... I... it was like a dream," Erika whispered, afraid.

"We should go, now," Doris demanded, but her legs were frozen solid to the spot. Even while she looked directly at her wife, she could feel the thing's gaze piercing her back. Her body locked her in fright, between the screaming instincts of fight or flight.

A piercing shriek started bellowing, rupturing her earlobes with hot pins, and Doris almost dropped the dog to cover her ears in a futile attempt to block it, but she was still frozen solid in dread. Erika's big, round eyes reflected elemental shadows in a starless night and Doris didn't want to turn around and see what was happening, how or why it was making that sound. Her wife opened her mouth and said something, but Doris couldn't hear it under the inhuman shriek. She could see two big tears of blood streaking out of Erika's ears, sliding over her slender neck and following the trail towards her collarbones.

Doris' brain shouted at her legs in revolt, and with a shot of adrenaline, she finally unstuck them from the spot; one hand wrapped around Erika and the other around the dog—dragging them away, all the while not turning around, not looking at the wailing thing in the sea.

It was only when they came to the house and she closed the front door—leaning against the wooden frame to catch her breath—that she noticed the wetness leaking from her own ringing ears.

Doris forced some food into her wife—the thin slices of prosciutto and hard cheese she found in the fridge, along with some moldy bread that father had probably bought precisely for them. Erika ate with a lost look, turned inwards, towards something only she was seeing. In Doris' mouth, each bite turned into acid, and she gagged with each morsel. She couldn't stop tasting rotten fish meat and salt, even when she was chewing cheese. But their bodies needed the energy, and her father didn't have much food, so it was better than none. Besides, she was pretty certain that whatever she put in her mouth would taste foul.

During all that time, her father stayed in his room, and the dog was lying corpse-still; she would've thought he'd died of exhaustion if not for the slow up and down movement of his chest. Her ears hurt like someone pierced them through with a needle, and she was afraid of the damage done to her eardrums. Sounds came to her through thick cotton, muffled and twisted. She should've let the damn dog limp right off the dock to the waiting sea creature, she thought bitterly. What was she trying to do here?

"Erika, what did you see?" Doris asked at one moment. Her eyes prickled with tears, but she refused to let them fall. She would not worry about her hearing at this point, about what it could mean moving forward. The inability to do her job wasn't even the scariest thing that could've happened, not at this point, so much as to lose what she held dear—the performance of sound she so cherished.

Erika touched her cheeks with trembling fingers, her face alight with a feverish glow. "The infinite vastness of the primordial sea." She enunciated each word loud and clear.

Doris felt better not knowing the answer.

At some point, she became aware of the time ticking away, the sunlight dimming in the cramped living room of her childhood home. Her father didn't show his face all this time, didn't come searching for food. Or water. In this sweltering weather, it was easy to dehydrate, and the fact she didn't check on him earlier weighed on her heart. So many things happened, all in one neverending day that felt stretched to eternity and back, and it was hard for her to stay upright. He could've died, she thought, maybe that's why he didn't descend or call to them. Maybe there was only a cooling corpse waiting for her to check up on him. Maybe it was the reason she was hesitating now.

With shaking hands, she picked up a jar of baby food and a glass of water and went upstairs, hollow ringing following her steps.

His room was engulfed in pitch-black darkness as if she'd opened the door to a cavern that never saw the light of day. The acidic smell of a decomposing body wafted out through the open doors. The raspy sounds of broken breathing ticked in her cotton-filled ears, and she couldn't be sure if she imagined them or if she could truly hear them. Somewhere in the room, two luminous small spheres suddenly twinkled in the dark. The reflecting eyes of a predator, her brain recognized, rippling her tender skin—from burning in the sun and, later, scratching herself clean of the dog's muck—in goosebumps.

"Dad?" she asked, sandpaper stuck in her throat. "I brought you something to eat. And drink."

The white orbs blinked away, then came back, closer. With a rush, her hand struck the wall and she hit the lightswitch. For an instant, her field of sight washed in the blinding light, and she could see the figure on the bed, leaning over towards her.

The gray ooze was coming out of his nose, covering his lower face in the dark liquid, sliding into his open mouth. His face was a collapsed grotto, the dark, round eyes the only thing bulging from the ruins. The grayness covered his whole head, making him look bloated. As if he'd been drowned while they weren't here, then brought back to life three days later.

"Dad?" An instinct told her to dash to his side; he was in pain and in desperate need of help. It urged her to try and clean up his face from the inky black goop streaming from his nostrils down his throat. Doris couldn't do that, couldn't make herself move even an inch closer to him, paralyised from the neck down, even when it made her feel like a heartless monster.

There were two parallel trails of dry dirt marking the path from his eyes to the chin, like he'd already cried the same thing out of them.

"I brought you food," she said, feeling dull, helpless. On the bed, her father gurgled. Where his mouth tried to shape words, bubbles popped in the petroleum-dark fluid. He leaned even further and spat out the goo with a loud wet sound.

"G... go... pl... plea..." She had to strain to hear him, both from the damage done to her and because of his difficulties with speaking. But she got the gist of it.

"I..." she said, uselessly standing in the doorway. *Do something*, she tried to command her brain. This didn't seem good. Bring Erika to help, clean him up the best that she can, and quickly drive him across the mountain, to the other side, to the nearest hospital.

Her arms moved and left the food and the water at the threshold. The figure on the bed blurred in colors and shapes, and Doris was startled to find that she was crying. Under the haze, she could see the shape of his head nodding, as if he was giving her a blessing to run away.

Doris moved away from the door, so she didn't need to see him, before collapsing on the floor and hugging her legs to her chest, letting out the sobs she'd tried to lock away behind a dam.

This story is a god-honest truth. It happened to a friend of a friend, I swear. That friend of a friend lived at the feet of an ancient god, sleeping in his rocky bed with clear skies above his heads. The god dreamed thousands of dreams of the people scattered over his vast body, but the man only dreamt of gold in the form of hundreds of untold tales. It was his passion that shaped his daughter's dreamscape, but it was the god who gave her the shape she desperately wanted, the one she knew was right for her. Why did the god do that, the man couldn't say, but it was a gift that formed an impassable wedge between him and his daughter who'd run away. Her tale became the only one he could never collect.

Doris listened to the story, sitting on the small wooden chair. The narrator was a wrinkled old man, one eye completely white from a cataract, but his voice was booming clear. He sounded like the wind rushing from the mountain to the sea, then breaking on the rooftops and narrow streets. Like the fog rolling over the trees, kissing the rocky teeth. He smelled like clean air and spring blooming over the valleys. The shadows around him danced, as if they were too afraid of touching him. His skin was alight with its own luminescence.

They were alone, and Doris felt like a child again. She turned to her left, then right, trying to find her father because, surely, he would not leave her alone with the storyteller. He would put her on his lap, or let her sit by his side, but never leave her alone, no matter where they visited, no matter how many people he knew in the village.

"He's not here, but you don't need to be afraid," the old man said and blinked away, like a breeze blowing a dandelion's fluff in the air. The dark descended on her with a hungry, enveloping hug, but she couldn't bear it, not again, please not again, before it retreated under a glowing light.

She was standing in the sea, hip deep. The cold water licked her skin, cooled her from the sweltering heat. Her mouth watered, wanting to drink it in. The sea had that crystal clear aquamarine color, and it made her weep.

"Don't cry over spilled milk," said her father, but it couldn't have been him. It was the old man, and yet, it wasn't the old man anymore, but a sea snake circling around her. "What's done, cannot be undone."

"What is going on here?" she asked the snake, but knew it was a futile gesture. It was not a snake, not a man, not a human in any comprehensible sense. It was something older and larger. Why was she even trying to reason with it? "Can you help him? Please? Like you did with me? I... don't know how to pray, but I can try."

The wind carried laughter on a cold breeze, chilling her upper body, where she stood in the sea.

"Why would we want to do that?"

"Why did you want to help me?" she finally said, afraid of the answer. So many people could only have the dreams and the wants they did because they lacked money, support, or chance. And her wishes got true because she was chosen by the well, by the god. "I haven't asked. I only fell asleep and woke up at the bottom of a dry well."

Stuck for days, for months, for years, at least it was what it felt like, with no one for company except the silent snake slithering in the dark—but when she truly got back to her body, she learned it had been the same night. But in the dream, it had been much longer than that. All the time she spent scaling the damp walls to the circular opening on the top, to the blazing white light promising escape, but her fingers constantly lost their grip and she would fall and fall and hit the rough, dry ground. It was an eternity of climbing, scratching, screaming, falling, hurt and despair until, finally, she managed to drag herself out of the well, to the warm cradle of the eternal darkness waiting behind the white veil. The darkness that broke her down to atoms, before putting her together like a jigsaw puzzle.

"Will you help him? I beg of you."

She hit the rocky bottom with her knees, the sea rising above her chest. If she had to call it a god and pray to it, she would. She alone could do nothing against the sickness that ravished her father, and nobody else seemed to care.

"Why do you think we could do that? What you had wished for in your heart was a part of nature, and we are nature. As is the caterpillar that cocoons, then breaks off like a butterfly. We just helped you along to achieve your metamorphosis, your true, natural self. But this is wrong. It's not natural. It's the opposite of natural."

"It's bacteria, and bacteria are nature," Doris argued.

"Don't be naive." The answer came from the sea this time, from the depths hidden from her view, from inside the closed pen shells rooted in the seabed.

"He's beyond our help. His transformation is already nearing the end. You can only choose two options now." Images flashed through her mind and new tears burst out, mingling with the sea. Salt from her body to the salt of the water. "And here's free advice, because we made you, rock-daughter, our butterfly-daughter; you deserve it. We will all die. We know that now. We see it coming to us, unavoidable, with the rushing tides of glowing red. It will eat our body and spit it out as something else. What, we do not know. But we saw what it did to the sea, and if it could do that to the cradle of life, we pose no threat to it. So whatever you choose to do, we hope that, in the end, you will run before it becomes too late. You should've never come back in the first place."

A bloody spill started spreading over the surface of the sea and something grabbed at her hands, dragging her underwater. Up and down changed, and she lost the seabed from her sight, drifting in the embrace of translucent ropes. Jellies swam all around her with bulbous, bell-like heads, slapping her face with their long, stinging tentacles. The vision of dark blue all around her started to change, scale over on the color spectrum into scarlet. There was no end to this boundless space, no horizons or skies or ground, just jellies floating in infinite space for all eternity, slowly eating her away to nothingness.

She woke up with a scream bursting from her chest,

her face sticky from crying, her clothes soaked in sweat. Her body was hurting, stiff from falling asleep fatigued on the hard ground of the upper floor, close to the room where her father was turning into soup without the protective layer of a cocoon. The hurt was a welcome feeling, grounding her to the reality she could handle. The one that had limits and clear boundaries.

The ancient being that was Velebit, the slumbering god that thought itself her other father, gave her two options to deal with the one waiting on his sickbed. A rock bashing through his skull until it turns to mush, or leaving him behind for whatever happens next. Doris didn't like either.

She wiped her tear-stricken face and went to search for her wife. Did Erika hear Doris scream? Did she even notice how much time passed while Doris slept on the floor? With fear gripping her heart, she descended the stairs and found Erika, rocking on the couch and looking at nothing at all.

Doris sat at the edge and enveloped Erika in a half hug, panic creeping over her. "Honey? Are you alright?"

Erika stopped in her motions and looked at Doris with shining wet eyes. "I can't forget it," she muttered. "Some say we came from the ground, and into the ground we'll go back, but we came from the sea. We came from the sea." Erika's teary eyes held such a focus on Doris that she felt she could drown in them just by watching. "And it wants us back."

CHAPTER 7

IT WANTS US BACK.

"I don't think there's an out in this," Erika whispered, face half-hidden behind the curtain of locs. She echoed the bleak message Doris got from the mountain. "Do you know what the scariest part of being stuck in the haunted čardak was?"

Doris gently caressed her back, her throat clogged with uncertainty. Erika, unlike Doris, who didn't like to talk about her time in the ninth well, didn't have any problems retelling her tale of supernatural misfortune, cracking jokes about it, or just thinking out loud about what it all might have meant. Searching for meaning. But Doris wasn't sure how to answer this question, and it was obviously meant as a rhetorical one, so she stayed silently supportive.

"Time didn't exist there," Erika continued. "Nothing was changing. I could feel this... void... this complete sense of stillness. I moved, I talked, but for my brain, I was in a state of stasis. I thought I would go mad." She turned her head towards Doris, brown eyes big and illuminated by the golden light of the lamp. "Everything's always changing, and if it weren't these strange bacteria, this strange creature, it would've been something else. But that's okay, we don't need to fear it."

"Honey, what are you talking about?" Doris said, her

ears ringing, her head on the verge of splitting from the headache. "You're not making much sense."

"You don't have to be afraid," Erika promised gravely, "we'll wait for it together. And your father, he'll be fine. He just needs to complete his change. Like you did." She leaned into Doris' half embrace. "It doesn't need to end in death. You saw it yourself. We could adapt, as we did before, when we crawled out of the primordial sea."

Doris blinked, the confusion over the events from the last few days slipping away. What Erika was talking about sounded... delirious. But not more than falling asleep with one set of organs and waking up with a different one. Not much more than the sight of drowned people in the sea, or people getting kidnapped by mountain fairies. It was different, unknown. Coming from the hidden places of the deep. And it was the future if one was to believe the mountain.

Her eyes fell on the sleeping dog, the gray scales on his ribs and tummy undulating under his haggard breath. They'd risked so much to get him back, but he wanted to go in there. To the creature that awaited him. She thought it had meant to eat the dog.

"I have an idea," Doris whispered to Erika, hugging her tighter. She kissed the top of her head. "But I'm scared." Scared of so many possibilities. Of accidentally killing her father. Of doing it on purpose. Of the future that was slowly reshaping the world that she knew and understood.

This new idea could end in disaster, but it was already too late for anything else. When her mother first called and begged her to come, she'd simply wanted a daughter and a father to reconcile. Erika had told Doris she should try and say goodbye to him before he died.

Both mother and Erika thought it would be easier for Doris to be here with him before his death, to see him for the last time while he still inhaled air. There was truth to that, but it also hurt deeply and without respite. With an intensity of an inflamed wound that had been left open to get infested with maggots burrowing deep inside the meat, eating her alive.

Her father had helped her clean herself after breaking out from her shell, and got rid of any evidence, so now she will do the same for him.

With a mask fixed on her face and cleaning gloves pulled on her hands, she stepped into the dark. He was watching her with two bulging eyes like a fish out of water, nostrils almost completely shut close with the newly growing patches of gray skin. She touched his shoulder and could feel heated lumps under her fingertips.

"I'm going to help you," she said through dried tears. "It's going to be alright. You don't need to be in pain anymore."

He gurgled in response, trying to form words through the phlegm amassed in his mouth, the blood mixed with a dense liquid, slowly trickling out of his lips and onto the floor. Whatever he wanted to tell her was lost, unintelligible. The inability to communicate will stay with them till the end.

That was the only regret she had. Not that she'd moved away—it was what she needed at the time, to be happy, and healthy, and move on. She could never regret the journey that ended with her meeting Erika, with the two of them living together, in love, married. But now, in this moment, watching the dark fluid dropping from her father's transforming mouth, seeing his lips getting shredded to pieces by the growth of gray scales, she felt the acute sadness of the fact that, in all these years, the two of them never found a way to talk, to understand each other, to connect.

She sat by his side on the bed, grasping his cold, clammy hand, covered in the greenish gray of a corpse.

"You're transforming," Doris whispered through her mask, breathing in the stale, filtered smell. "There's nothing wrong with that." It was a lie spoken aloud, but she hoped it sounded sincere and kind.

His eyes narrowed, and even in the inhuman face, she could read the disbelief in them. He raised the hand she wasn't holding and touched his chest. Asking a question she didn't really understand.

"We can't stop this. No one can," Doris said, letting sadness out with each word, with each breath. "I saw the... god," she confessed, the word tasting wrong on her tongue, dissatisfactory. But he will understand what she meant to say. "They said so. There's no fixing this."

More gurgling sounds, this time more pronounced, more frantic. Her father wanted to say something, maybe to object, maybe to plead, but it all got drowned in the waste of his lungs. Of his insides.

She choked on the tears welling in her throat. "It'll be alright. Relax, relax, shhh." As if he were a child, she rocked him gently in her arms, consoling him while he threw up blood, bile, and tissue. Through all of it, he made keening sounds, fat tears dropping from his eyes and mingling with vomit. Gently, Doris caressed his head and felt his spongy skin under her gloves.

"I will help you through this, as you helped me, a long time ago," she whispered, uncaring if he could hear her or not. Her father was a part of her journey from the beginning, never doubting her transition, ever since she'd come out to him and mother as a child. There was never any doubt about them being on her side. Even before an ancient power took it into its hands to intervene in her life in such a dramatic way.

Daughter of the mountain. Daughter of the well. The lost treasure, held in captivity by the snake. In the folk tale, her father would've been the one to save her from the darkness, kissing the snake on top of its head so it would release her from the well. But it hadn't happened. He hadn't been sharing that dream. She'd been alone in the darkness, until she'd fought to get out, all by herself.

Maybe he hadn't been there to save her, but he had been there before and after.

She hadn't come back here to save him. But she could be with him. Until the end.

Helping him out of the bed, painstakingly slow and half dragging him like a dead weight, she managed to get them out of the room. The sun has already set, and bioluminescence will shine its way through the town. She didn't want anyone to see them. She didn't want their scientist neighbors to know something was going on. Doris wasn't certain if it was more out of fear they might try to stop her, or out of concern they might whip out their equipment to document everything as some kind of scientific curiosity. To help them advance their research. To take him from her and safely tuck him away in some kind of aquarium, hooked to the machines, with a neurolink inserted under the scaly flesh. Ironically, only the day before—or was it hours before?—she was angry that her father didn't want to be in a lab, undergoing experiments like a helpful little lab rat.

Her father wasn't that heavy anymore, so much of

his body fat and mass already devoured. It felt as if he were made of nothing but water, kept in place by stretched-out, scaly skin. He wobbled on his feet, unable to hold himself upright without her help. Like two drunks, they almost dropped down into the living room.

Erika was kneeling by the dog, her hand on his chest.

"Is he—"

"He's breathing, but shallow. He won't..." Erika inhaled and shook her head before turning toward Doris and her father. "We should go. Do you need help?"

"No. You take the dog."

The night was washed in the red of blood, of birth and death. Cats crawled out from the underbrush, jumped on the trash cans, and came from the ruined fortress, hissing at them, with their fur electrified and their eyes filled with hunger. They followed the somber procession but didn't dare to come near. Doris was dragging her father; he was still gurgling something and slobbering foul liquid all over her shoulder. In her ears, she could still hear a slight ringing, as if someone were incessantly drumming in the rhythm of their steps. The town held its breath watching them go through it, dread brewing in the bricks and cement, under its narrow streets. Shutters resembled eyelids sewn shut, but she could still feel the focused attention from the windows, following their passage. Even if there was no one living there. The houses remembered her and knew her father. They were silent witnesses to the great metamorphosis of humankind.

Once the sea level rises, they, too, will join them under. Maybe her father will get to live in his house again one day. Maybe he'll get to float with his ruined books and hard disks, with the jellies lighting the way.

The closer they got to the glowing crimson water,

the more her father started to trash in her hands. Doris wasn't sure if he wanted them to go faster or to run away, but she kept her grip on him. Silent tears slipped down her cheeks, soaking her mask. Blurring her vision, as if she were already underwater.

He slipped and they both almost fell to the ground. His arm stretched out, pointing across the road, towards the sea. His eyes shone, reflecting the red light.

"Yes, we're close," she answered the question she thought he was asking. There was a buzzing in the air, mixing with the ringing in her ears. Doris helped her father up again, tired, angry, confused, hurting, but most of all sad. With resolve, she clenched her jaw and dragged him a few steps more, over the road, towards the beach. Erika followed behind, the unnaturally calm dog in her arms.

The sea was undulating before Doris' eyes as if under a wind she couldn't feel. The surface level of jellies was aflame. Doris had thought they were all dying, like her father, but now she understood that they had just been changed. In this moment, illuminating the night brighter than the stars, they were more alive than she felt. They were dancing, expanding and shrinking, one over the other, forming one gigantic pulsating organ. The beating heart of the sea.

The ringing in her ears intensified.

Her father flailed in her arms and she gently lowered him to the ground. She could've just rolled him over the edge of the concrete, let him fall and hit the waiting water. But she couldn't be sure where the rocks were under the clusters of the jellies, and he could still bash his head open on them. And besides, it was undignified, to be rolled over like a log.

Instead, first she stripped him of his clothes,

exposing to the air and her eyes the mushy gray body as if he were turning into a human-shaped sponge. His moans intensified and she finally saw through the hole of his mouth. All of his teeth had fallen off, the meat completely raw, red, and empty. But under the red illumination, there was a glimpse of something bulging from the toothless gums. New teeth will grow out, sharp and pointy, in more rows than humanly possible. *It will all be alright*, she told him with her eyes. He was shaking his head, tears still leaking from his beady eyes.

She wiped away his tears with the same, calming motion he'd used when he was cleaning the blood, tears, and muck away from her face.

He'd cried too, she remembered. As they were both crying now.

"You're becoming something more. You're going to become what you've always loved!" she yelled through her mask, over the buzzing in her ears, to be certain he could hear her. "A tale!" She hugged his trembling body and waited for a bit for him to calm down.

"Doris," Erika called to her with a warning tone. Doris followed her wife's gaze to the spot in the sea where, in the midst of the gleaming jellies, a head bobbed, with vivid coals for eyes, and a round, saw-like mouth. It was waiting too. Will it try to eat her father when she lowers him to the sea? The stronger predators feed on the weaker, isn't that the case? Or was it waiting for another of its kind, to help him navigate the change and to adapt to new rules? To teach him how to hunt.

There was no turning back, she knew. Her father will have to learn to do some things on his own. To survive. To fight if he has to. There was always a limit to how much one could help.

With the approach of the creature, her father finally

calmed. Did he recognize his future or did he simply give up? Either way, he let her gently carry him over to the remaining stairs leading to the sea. Carefully, she chose the stone fragments still sturdy and big enough for her feet, until there was no more rock for her to stand on. At that point, she lowered him to the surface and gently let go. And he complied, slipping inside the cover of jellies. The splash was so quiet she almost missed it under the buzzing sounds. His head disappeared under the dense little bodies. The creature dove under too, the jellies on its head rippling slightly where it broke the surface. The sea ate them away and she stood on the precipice, hanging only by a thread.

Erika came to her side and crouched, lowering her own offering to the sea. The small bundle of scales and fur broke through the cluster of jellies, only to slide underneath, as a pebble dropped into the water.

Jellies closed down above him, just like they did after her father's descent. Whatever was happening right now was hidden from their view by the red curtain of bioluminescence and a blanket made of living gelatine. The surface calmed as if the sea were satisfied.

Erika put a hand over Doris' shoulder, grasping tight.

Doris turned her head towards the distant sky, hoping to see the stars and the moon over the haze of scarlet, looking down on them in this moment of solitude and grief. Instead, she finally saw what was making the awful buzzing sound she'd thought existed only in her ears.

The drone hung over their heads, an unwelcome witness to the intimate family farewell.

EPILOGUE

THE BOAT ROCKED SLIGHTLY, but not as much as it used to do when the sea was clear. Jellies cushioned it to the spot, making their advance slow as if they were moving through a dense pudding. Erika brought down the peddle, sweat breaking out on her forehead with each push. But there was no way they would use the engine, the blades of which could turn the living jellies into soup.

So, they were rowing. Through a burning ache in their hands, but content with their progress.

They didn't have to go too far from the beach. In the beginning, they didn't need to go out on the sea at all. But the more the red stretched towards the Pag island, the more *they* followed. And once the bacteria had finally eaten its way through to Pag's coast, it was harder to bring *them* back. They followed the expansion for food, after all. For whatever reason, they disliked the clean sea, or couldn't survive too long there. So first the bacteria had to eat and infest, to start the change, and then the rest of the colony followed.

Something suddenly hit the bottom of the boat, making them rock harder. A head ascended from the jellies, two glowing eyes and a snout with polyps hanging from it like whiskers. Stribor didn't look like a dog anymore, not even like a seal. Something in between, with razor-sharp teeth. He always came first.

Doris patted him on his head. "Good boy," her mouth formed the words by instinct. He tried to bite her hand, but she was faster, as always. Instead, she threw a piece of store-bought meat overboard, raw and thawed.

It was also getting harder to get the food—no one was willing to deliver groceries to the dead town with two living residents. She had to drive all the way to Senj or even Rijeka to buy food in the quantities they needed. For Erika and her. For the others. Money was also getting tighter. But before they'd figured out that the bacteria had spread to Pag—so much for the nano filters that were supposed to prevent that—there had been troubling news of overturned boats and missing fishermen and tourists. While no one saw what had happened, Doris and Erika had their suspicions, so they didn't want to risk it, starting these feeding rituals instead.

Her mother didn't understand what they were doing. Didn't understand why they didn't get back to their jobs and their lives. Thought it was some sort of trauma related to the disappearance of Doris' father, a presumed suicide to everyone else. Doris didn't know how to explain what happened, and after some time she stopped.

No matter where they went, they wouldn't be able to run away. To leave this behind. Not since Erika had gazed upon the primordial sea, glimpsed the future ahead.

They will all understand one day, though. Doris wasn't surprised when she'd heard that the infected people outside of the town were dying in pools of melted organs, suffocating like fish out of water. Some had come back, following an instinct inside of them, and those found Erika and her, willing to help them to cross over to the new life. But what did surprise Doris, though it shouldn't have, was the news that the bacteria were found near the coast of Florida. They hadn't spread there on their own, certainly. Their movement towards Pag was slow, deliberate. But just because something was slow on its own, it didn't mean it couldn't be spread faster, either by negligence, or a deliberate choice.

If she had to guess whose hand had played a role in this turn of events, she would've put her money on the research team they had met. She should've fed them to her father and the creature. But in those days, she was mostly afraid they would try to fish her father out, so when she saw them, one morning, packing up their stuff, she was relieved just to see them go away.

Chloe had tried to apologize to her before she went in the van, but Doris only asked, again, did she know what was in the sea?

"I wasn't lying when I told you I didn't know," Chloe had said. "We only saw... glimpses... of something impossible. Always moving away. Too fast. But Rowan believed this was the reason all of this was happening and if we just caught it, we'd be able to understand the process underway," Chloe had whispered to her, confidentially, and Doris had wondered if the two of them would've been friends in other circumstances. "Rowan became obsessed... and tried to do that on her own, but never came back. As you know."

It was the parting gift, this admission before Chloe got in the navy blue van and disappeared from their life.

Doris didn't want to believe Chloe had anything to do with the spread of the bacteria on the Florida coast, but they were the only ones here, taking samples, taking something else from below. It was the logical conclusion.

"It's fine, it'll be faster this way," was the only thing Erika had to say about all of that.

Another bump against the boat, on the other side this time. Leon's splotchy head rose above the surface. No matter how much they changed, there was always a hint of resembling who they were before. She dropped him a whole chicken and he took it in his round, open mouth with delight. Her wife looked at her and signed along the lines of, "It will not be enough for everyone if you're this generous. Let them fight over it if they have to."

After hearing enough of the screams from the townsfolk—what her wife called their sea song, for when they were particularly angry or happy—too much damage was done to their eardrums to be able to hear anything. But it wasn't important. Erika and she could still communicate, learning Croatian sign language from the net in all the free time they had.

It made buying food and other necessities more difficult, but not impossible. The worst thing was to walk among the people of Rijeka, the big crowds she knew produced all sorts of sounds, and be unable to hear them. Only feel the town's vibrations. To not be able to hear someone perform a tale of long ago, like she'd used to when she was a child. She hadn't cared about her work for a long time, but she cared about that at least.

The thing that made her the saddest, however, was that her father wouldn't get the tale he deserved. One told by a town elder to the gathered people. Instead, his story existed as a video filmed by a drone, most probably shown to unconcerned corporate people. But maybe the remaining townsfolk, living under the sea, now had their own way of performing folk tales. Maybe he managed to keep the tradition alive, now transformed into something else.

More heads dove out, more gaping, hungry mouths.

The mountain hadn't tried to communicate with her anymore. If it was disappointed by her decision to stay, or if it had simply given up on life and gone back to its slumber, she didn't know. But from that side, the weirdness had stopped, as it knew the time had come for the sea to birth new legends.

It wasn't all that bad, she thought, dropping the food across the sides of the boat. The sea was the best bet for the survival of humanity, wasn't it? Who knows what was the reason why Chloe's shady employer had sent them, or what could be the motivation to release this thing at home. Maybe to find a way to adapt to the new world, while they destroyed the old.

It didn't matter anymore. There was something unburdening in the knowledge that this was unavoidable. Erika and she spent their days tangled on the bed or at the beach, without a care in the world. Without grief and guilt. It was all pointless, faced with the vastness of the sea.

Her father came to the boat, catching its side with his clawed hand. She put her palm over his, ignoring how clammy and cold his skin was to the touch. Under the blooming light of dawn, the patch of gray growth covering her forearm glistened.

Life was unspooling towards the end. Not with a bang, or a whimper, but with a splash.

They will all go back.

And the sea was waiting for them with its arms wide open.

ACKNOWLEDGMENTS

First, thank you, dear reader, for giving this book of mine a chance in the sea of other amazing books. I hope, if you've come to this point, that you had a good time. If you have a moment, and the energy, please consider leaving a review on Goodreads, The StoryGraph, your retailer of choice, or wherever you like leaving reviews and comments. I'm not a well-known author, and Shtriga is a micro publishing company, so word of mouth goes a long way to help this book reach its audience.

Second, as always, big thanks to my partner in crime Vesna, who wanted to get into the publishing business with me, and who endures my writing. Without her editing input and constant support, I honestly don't think I would be here where I'm now, productivity- and publishing-wise. She also didn't kill me over what I did to the dog, so thanks for that, too!

To Antonio Filipović, my cover artist, goes the biggest thanks of all! He's amazing and sweet, and his art is really cool. I didn't have a lot of ideas about what to put on the cover (only that it had to be red), so I gave him free reign, and in the end, he picked three amazing scenes for his sketches—it was hard to choose. We went with this one, and given the first reactions after we revealed the cover, we weren't wrong to do so. To see more of his awesome work, please go visit his IG page @a.th.a.n.

I would also like to thank a NaNo friend and fellow writer, Iluzija O. Istini, who for sure didn't expect that her infographic on the jellyfish in the Adriatic, or her explanation that comb jellies aren't actually medusas because they don't have stingrays, would in any way be influential or inspirational for my writing. I was actually so amazed by the infographic that I started writing aquatic horror (instead of working on my urban fantasy novel), but the primary idea I had just didn't work, and I had to scratch it. In the end, the jellies managed to find a way to this novella, in a different way.

Lastly, I want to thank Steve Stred and Ladies of Horror Fiction, who facilitate the LoHF Writers Grant for women writers of horror. I got the grant in 2021, and the money went into partially financing this novella. They, and all the authors and publishers who donated to the grant, rock, and I was more than honored to get it. (I almost didn't apply). It helped not just financially, but also motivationally, every time I hit a wall while writing. So thank you for giving me a chance.

AUTHOR'S NOTE

I had one pretty big problem: whether to name the town in this novella or not. I talked a lot with Vesna about it. Given what happens to the town, we felt that maybe it wouldn't be best to leave the name in, and for a bit, I played with the idea of writing about it with the initial, just K., like some old-timey gothic story. The other version was calling it 'the town', but that would've become tiring pretty early on. And what would be the point? It's not like I was inspired by Karlobag, but then wrote about a similar, though imaginary town. There were too many recognizable features to hide the fact—the placement, the half-church with the graveyard, the ruined fortress. So, we decided we would keep the name, even though this book is not its best promo material.

I was inspired to write this novella last summer, when visiting Karlobag, and the place itself was inextricably linked to the plot, so that's the reason I wanted it for the setting of my folk-flirting-with-aquatic-horror tale. It wasn't just about any coastal town—it was about that particular one. Because I liked that half-church, the derelict changing rooms, the fortress and the cats (yes, there's a lot of them!), and all the 'Bikers Welcome' signs. I also like how it's a twenty minute ride from the town to a part of the Velebit mountain where one can go on an easy (or hard) hike. It's perfect. And depressing. The part about the highway screwing it over is very much true. It's not an easy life there, or so I've heard. But it's a nice place, with interesting history, and even though the sea is really cold, it's a good place to visit.

I don't actually have a grudge against tourists, until I see the food prices on the coast. Joking aside, there are a lot of problems with rich tourists renting out speedboats for their joyrides without much thought for the other boats, the swimmers and the divers. The amount of accidents at sea and diver deaths... is depressing. And the frequency of tourists losing their lives on Velebit is also, unfortunately, correct (and not just there: at other hills and mountains too). There are a lot of... inappropriate jokes about flip flops, so much so that even our mountain rescue service joined in on at one point, to raise awareness of it through the power of memes.

When I decided to set a story in Karlobag, I researched the local folktales and legends, thinking there had to be, for sure, something sea-related to be used, because I wanted to write an aquatic horror, but I also like folklore a lot and wanted to combine it. I was wrong, though, but found a great paper analyzing folk tales of the places in Velebit's foothills. The tales collected were hilarious (the werewolf, for example, is a waterskin filled with blood, rolling down the road) and I had a lot of fun reading them. Even though the truth behind them wasn't as fun. The story of the ninth well is recorded exactly as presented here, and for the reason stated here (poverty). But I didn't like the heteronormativity of it (*oh, there's this hidden treasure, and sometimes there's an imprisoned girl, and the guy dreaming of it can save her*), so of course I couldn't have that. The idea, *but oh, what if the dreamer is actually a trans girl and the imprisoned girl is herself, and she saves herself,* flashed in my mind and the rest is... well, this book.

But I'm not a trans woman. I only like writing about women, and that includes all of them (so it's not even my first trans woman protagonist). But I can't talk about the trans experience, and that wasn't my intention. If you want to read about trans women protagonists in queer horror written by trans women, I can recommend a few: *Transmuted* by Eve Harms (a body horror novella that's one hell of a ride), *The Worm and His Kings* by Hailey Piper (excellent cosmic horror novella), *Tell Me I'm Worthless* by Alison Rumfitt (a gut-wrenchingly raw haunted house novel), and of course, *Manhunt* by Gretchen Felker-Martin (a brilliant post-apocalypse novel).

These are just the few titles that delve into a trans woman's experience in queer horror, written by trans women, that I've read, but I also want to point out there are so many amazing trans writers out there, writing all sorts of queer horror.

I feel in love with indie queer horror scene, and my reading is definitely better for it.

My only hope is that I can give something back with my writing, and to write exactly the type of the book someone was looking for.

ABOUT THE AUTHOR

Antonija Mežnarić is a Croatian writer and editor, who lives and breathes speculative fiction. She loves to write queer horror and urban fantasy inspired by folklore. Alongside her partner, she runs a small Croatian publishing house Shtriga, she's the co-editor at the online magazine for speculative fiction Morina kutija (morinakutija.com), and a co-host of the Croatian podcast about writing and publishing, Mora FM.

Her notable works include the sapphic horror comedy novella What Do Nightmares Dream of and a queer folk horror collection Mistress of Geese.

You can follow her book ramblings on hauntednarratives.com or on Instagram and Twitter @antonijamezni.

ALSO BY ANTONIJA

WHAT DO NIGHTMARES DREAM OF

There's someone else living in Sanja's flat and they don't pay the rent. But for Sanja, the next time she falls asleep she just might end up paying the ultimate price.

Sanja has already made some hard choices in life. She took out a loan to get her own place for the first time ever, and now she's repaying it by working at the most ungrateful job in history: elementary school teacher.

The last thing she needs is her nightmares to start tormenting her, as if her grandmother's special breed of childcare wasn't enough.

In a world that doesn't believe in old wives' tales, her options are limited. It's now up to her to deal with her supernatural pest or forever fall asleep trying.

A sapphic horror comedy novella about loneliness, anxiety and a tired teacher trying to live with a nightmare creature.

MISTRESS OF GEESE

Mistress of Geese is a collection of folk horror tales about isolation, loneliness, destructive powers of nature, magic and creatures lurking in the dark.

The undiscovered, occasionally almost uninhabited remote areas of the old European land of Croatia hold secrets only the bravest of women can find. The only question is, will they survive the discovery or be taken into darkness as the land demands?

One dring that turns a fun scifi convention into a nightmarish fight for survival. A lottery held for maiden sacrifice so the toxic rain can stop in a magical post-apocalypse. A dream vacation going horribly wrong because sometimes the past is better left alone. A curse on a small town and a reluctant hero who has to break it. A secret legacy and ancient gods clashing over the head of a lonely girl living in an insatiable forest...

Are you ready to follow the geese?

ABOUT SHTRIGA

Hidden Stories In Your Pocket.
Sci-fi, fantasy and horror on the go. Publishing your daily dose of speculative fiction since 2020.

Visit shtriga.com for more information. Follow us on Twitter, Instagram and Facebook @shtrigabooks.

Or subscribe to our newsletter Centipede News!

SHTRIGA

www.ingramcontent.com/pod-product-compliance
Lightning Source LLC
Chambersburg PA
CBHW071626150726
48000CB00004B/1902